Sweet 16

PRAISE FOR KATE BRIAN

The Princess & the Pauper

"Romance, action, adventure, and large doses of humor . . . fun and fast-paced." —*VOYA*

"Compulsively readable." —*Horn Book Guide*

"Entertaining." —*Publishers Weekly*

"A great book for the . . . girl who loves romance as well as empowerment." —*Romantic Times Book Club*

The V Club

"Truly exceptional chick lit." —*Kirkus Reviews*

"It's about wanting to grow up and knowing when you are (or are not) ready to do so." —www.teenreads.com

"A good read for high school girls." —*VOYA*

"A feel-good message about remaining true to oneself." —*Publishers Weekly*

"Explore[s] the complex relationships of four very different girls trying to make good choices about sex, secrets, and speaking up . . . and their dreams for the future." —*Bulletin of the Center for Children's Books*

Lucky T

"A fabulous new novel for the nomad in any teen." —*Midwest Book Review*

"Well written, with . . . suspense and comedy." —*Kirkus Reviews*

"Another wonderful summer travel book." —*Romantic Times Book Club*

"Young teen girls who liked Ann Brashares's *The Sisterhood of the Traveling Pants* will enjoy this book."

—*VOYA*

"This exciting tome will keep you rooting for the heroine until the very last page!" —*Wow!*

Megan Meade's Guide to the McGowan Boys
"[S]trong characterizations lift this above formula . . . fans of Brian's *The V Club* will want to read this." —*Booklist*

"[F]ans . . . will enjoy the escapism." —*Kirkus Reviews*

by
KATE BRIAN

SIMON & SCHUSTER BOOKS FOR YOUNG READERS
New York   London   Toronto   Sydney

SIMON & SCHUSTER BOOKS FOR YOUNG READERS
An imprint of Simon & Schuster Children's Publishing Division
1230 Avenue of the Americas, New York, New York 10020
This book is a work of fiction. Any references to historical
events, real people, or real locales are used fictitiously. Other
names, characters, places, and incidents are products of the
author's imagination, and any resemblance to actual events or
locales or persons, living or dead, is entirely coincidental.

SIMON & SCHUSTER BOOKS FOR YOUNG READERS is a trademark
of Simon & Schuster, Inc.

Produced by Alloy Entertainment

 151 West 26th Street

New York, NY 10001

Book design by Joel Tippie
The text for this book is set in New Baskerville.
Manufactured in the United States of America

2 4 6 8 10 9 7 5 3

Library of Congress Cataloging-in-Publication Data
Brian, Kate, 1974–
Sweet 16 / Kate Brian.— 1st ed.
p. cm.
Summary: On the night of her sweet sixteen birthday party, self-centered
snob Teagan Phillips receives a visit from a special person who tries to
convince the teenager to change the way she lives her life.
ISBN-13: 978-1-4169-0032-0
ISBN-10: 1-4169-0032-2
[1. Self-perception—Fiction. 2. Conduct of life—Fiction. 3. Birthdays—Fiction.
4. Parties—Fiction.] I. Title: Sweet sixteen. II. Title.
PZ7.B75875Swe 2006
[Fic]—dc22   2005020550

Special thanks to Lynn Weingarten for always just getting it

Interview with Teagan Phillips re:
Upcoming Sweet Sixteen Party
Transcript 1

Reporter: Melissa Bradshaw, Senior Editor,
Rosewood Prep Sentinel

MB: This is Melissa Bradshaw, reporting for
the Rosewood Prep Sentinel. I'm here with
Teagan Phillips, sophomore, who is going to
chat with us about what may be one of the most
anticipated parties of the year, her upcoming
sweet sixteen. So, Teagan, tell me, why
should the Sentinel run a story about your
sweet sixteen?

TP: (*pause*) You want me to *convince* you?

MB: Well, Rosewood Prep is an exclusive
school, as you well know. We have at least
three huge blowouts a month. What makes yours
so special? Why should we feature it instead
of, say, Donnie Darko's graduation party?

TP: (*clears her throat*) Well, *Missy*, first of
all, Donald Moskowitz renamed himself after a
cult film character who talks to psychotic
murderous bunnies that hang out in his bedroom. So let's just say that his little fete
is likely to include a massive murder-suicide
plot, while mine is going to be the most exclusive, the most fabulous, the most intense

party this school has ever seen. Which would *you* rather attend, Missy?

MB: It's Melissa, actually. So, let me get this straight, you're claiming that your party is going to be better than, say, Chad Reilly's all-senior weekend in the Bahamas?

TP: Please. People talked about that cheese-a-palooza for what? A month? They're going to be talking about this one for *years*.

MB: Interesting . . . interesting. So you've been working on this party for how long?

TP: Over twelve months.

MB: And how many other sweet sixteens have you attended in that time?

TP: Oh, at least fifteen.

MB: And have you been taking notes?

TP: (*scoffs*) Hardly. Unless you count the mile-long list of things *not* to do. My sweet sixteen is going to blow those lame fests out of the water.

MB: So am I to understand that all this work you've done on this little soiree is motivated by sheer competitive drive?

TP: You bet your [edited for content] it is.

Chapter 1

"Mrs. Natsui!"

Teagan Phillips was thirty seconds into her day and already she was seriously pissed off. She sat up straight in her four-poster bed, her silk rose-colored Calvin Klein nightgown twisted around her size-six body like a straitjacket, and shouted at the top of her lungs.

"Mrs. Natsui! Get your ass in here!"

Teagan jabbed at the buttons on her remote control, flipping the channels on her plasma-screen TV until it finally landed on the Weather Channel. A snarky-looking guy with a clipped white mustache grinned back at her from behind his state-of-the-art weather desk.

"And it's a washout for the greater Philadelphia area today," he said as the screen snapped to live shots of the Liberty Bell, the steps outside the art museum, and the Pennsylvania Turnpike. Windshield wipers whipped furiously and raindrops pelted the camera lenses. "We're looking at record rainfall and possibly some thunderstorms rolling in late today, lasting straight through the night. If you live anywhere in eastern Pennsylvania or southern New Jersey, you're gonna want to break out your golf umbrellas and galoshes, people. It's gonna be a wet one!"

Teagan groaned and hit the power button. Slumping over her bunched-up hand-knit cashmere blanket, she stared across her cavernous bedroom to the bay window that over-looked the gardens and pool in the backyard. The sky was so dark it could have been nine at night instead of nine o'clock in the morning. The rain battered the perennials in her win-dow boxes, beating them down. It should have been a beauti-ful, sunny spring day. The birds should have been chirping. The windows should have been open and a light breeze should have been tickling the gold chiffon curtains that flut-tered around her bed. It should have been perfect. It was *supposed* to be perfect.

Teagan sucked in as much air as her lungs would hold and raised her voice to the rafters. "*Mrs.! Nat! Su! Iiiiiii!!!!*"

"Good morning, Miss Teagan!" Mrs. Natsui trilled as she padded into the room in her stiff black uniform and black sneakers. There was some sort of yellow stain on her white apron. Her graying hair was clipped back at the nape of her neck and she wore her humongous, red-rimmed glasses attached to her neck by a gold chain. She clutched a huge bouquet of colorful balloons in both hands and had an incred-ibly wide smile on. "Happy birthday!"

"Yeah, right," Teagan said, whipping the eight-hundred-thread-count Egyptian cotton sheets aside and stuffing her feet into her new sheepskin Coach slippers. "Why the hell didn't you tell me it was going to rain today?"

She trudged over to the window, yanking at her twisted nightie, and shoved aside the wispy curtain. Outside, the lush green grass was dotted with thick, muddy puddles as far as the eye could see. Budding trees bent under the force of the wind. The pelting rain made pockmarks in the sparkling pool water, which was peppered with white petals ripped from a nearby dogwood. All the lounge chairs had been removed and stashed inside the storage area of the pool house, which meant that at the very least the landscaping staff had known about the downpour ahead of time. Somebody should have warned her. Wasn't it kind of their job?

"I'm sorry, Miss Teagan," Mrs. Natsui said. "But what does the weather matter on such a special day? Your sweet sixteen!"

Try soaked sixteen, Teagan thought, just imaging the stupid puns her friends were going to make. This was unbelievable. Today was supposed to be the biggest day of her life. She had been looking forward to it *forever*. Today was the day she was supposed to have the party to end all sweet sixteen parties. The party that was going to totally kick the butt of Shari Marx's lame aloha-themed debacle with its pork kabobs and tacky plastic leis. She had spent weeks planning the event all the way down to the very last detail, spending her father's money like it was tap water in order to make sure everything was perfect. Over two hundred people had RSVP'd, the very crème de la crème of suburban Philadelphia society. Today was the day Teagan Phillips was going to prove to the world that she was the most stylish, wealthy, doted-upon girl in Upper Sheridan, Pennsylvania.

Or at least the one who knew how and where to spend the most cash.

But how was she supposed to have an elegant cocktail

hour on the slate patio of the country club if the patio in question was submerged in water?

"Look! Look what that fancy school of yours has sent for you!"

Mrs. Natsui brought the balloon bouquet over to the window. Teagan tore the card from the ribbons and scanned it quickly.

Happy sweet sixteen to one of our top students! Best wishes, the faculty and staff of Rosewood Prep.

Teagan looked up at the balloons. They really were kind of pretty. When she was little, balloons had been her favorite part of any birthday party. Her mother had always ordered so many helium balloons they crowded out the ceiling. Super-long ribbons were attached to each one, long enough for the kids to grab at and twirl around their fingers. Teagan had loved the way the ribbons curled down and tickled her cheeks wherever she walked.

A squishy lump of sorrow formed in Teagan's chest and she scoffed, letting the balloons go until they bounced up to her cathedral ceiling and got entangled in the whirring ceiling fan.

"They're just fishing for another donation," she said, turning her attention back to the deluge outside.

"Oh!" Mrs. Natsui exclaimed, rushing for the switch on the wall to turn off the fan. It made an ominous-sounding squeal and finally sputtered and died. A couple of balloons popped, sandwiched between the fan blades and the stucco ceiling.

"God! Are you *trying* to give me a heart attack?" Teagan asked, flattening her hand against her chest.

"Of course not, Miss Teagan," Mrs. Natsui said.

Teagan rolled her eyes, then glared at the clouds outside. She pulled her thick brown hair over her shoulder and examined it. Yep. Just as she suspected. It was already pulling a Chia pet. Why couldn't her father have settled in LA or Arizona? Someplace arid and far, far away from this nightmare humidity.

Michel better be on top of his game today, she thought, already picturing her stylist's horrified face when he got a look at her 'fro. He would just have to earn his tip, that was all. There was no way Teagan was showing up at her sweet sixteen looking like a Muppet.

"I will send David up to deal with that," Mrs. Natsui said, gesturing to the ceiling.

"Think we could refrain from calling in the staff peeping Tom until *after* I'm dressed?" Teagan asked.

Mrs. Natsui sighed but got to work making Teagan's bed without another word. Teagan slumped onto the window seat, pressing her forehead against the clear glass, absently picking at her fingernails. She knew she should hit the shower already and get on with her day, but all she felt like doing at that moment was crawling back into bed. What had she done to deserve this? Did the universe really hate her this much?

Her stomach grumbled and Teagan put her hand over it. Not that Natsui would ever notice or that Teagan cared a smidge what the woman thought of her. Teagan just detested bodily functions of any kind and hated being reminded that she even had a stomach. Especially after last night's peanut M&M fest.

She had known when she tore into that party-size bag that karma would find a way of getting back at her. But what was she supposed to do? It was the night before her birthday, she

was all alone, her boyfriend, Max Modell, hadn't even bothered to call her before going on his underage bar crawl in
Philly, and, as always was the case the night before her birthday, she couldn't stop thinking about her mom. Teagan had
responded to all this adversity in the only way she knew how.
She had turned on the *Newlyweds: Nick and Jessica* rerun
marathon and downed the whole bag of chocolate before Nick
had even once rolled his eyes behind Jessica's back.

Eating the M&M's made her feel less anxious. But digesting them was another story. Digesting them made her feel like
a fat pig. How many calories were in an entire bag of peanut
M&M's? She could already feel her hips expanding.

But wasn't that punishment enough? Didn't she get any
sympathy points from whoever was in charge of karma for
being a half orphan? Did they really have to hit her with a
monsoon? It was just so unfair.

"You should get dressed, Miss Teagan," Mrs. Natsui said,
expertly placing one of a half dozen silk-and-ribbon throw pillows on Teagan's bed. "Miss Karen is downstairs waiting for you."

Teagan blew out an exasperated sigh and rolled her eyes.
A perfect start to a perfect day.

"What does *she* want?" Teagan asked, heading for her
walk-in closet, her slippers sinking into the plush carpet.

"She wants to wish you a happy birthday, Miss Teagan,"
Mrs. Natsui replied.

Alone in the walk-in, which was more the size of a small
bedroom, Teagan mouthed Mrs. Natsui's words, making an
irritated face. "*She wants to wish you a happy birthday, Miss
Teagan.*" Wasn't it against the rules for the help to condescend
to her? She shoved aside one designer dress after another,
looking for something to wear to the salon.

Why does Karen insist on trying to bond with me? she thought, irritated. *You've got the rock on your finger! Congratulations! You don't have to pretend to like me anymore!*

Finally Teagan grabbed a cashmere V-neck sweater by Nicole Miller—black to match her mood—and her favorite Seven jeans—the ones that downplayed her butt and made her look super-skinny. She opened one of her dozen lingerie drawers and took out a set of lacy black La Perla underwear. Expensive, sophisticated lingerie always made her feel more elegant and sure of herself. At this point, she could use all the help she could get. Before she walked out of the closet, she slid her fingers down the silk paisley Gucci scarf that hung on a hook next to the door—an old ritual.

On her way to her private bathroom, Teagan grabbed her pink cell phone from her vanity table and turned it on. Immediately the phone beeped, indicating she had a message. Teagan dropped her clothes on the velvet-covered bench inside her bathroom and hit the message button.

She smiled for the first time all day when she heard Max's voice.

"Hey, Sweet Bottom! Just calling to say good night! Miss you already," Max said as his friends cackled and hooted in the background. The smile faded when she realized he was totally trashed and way beyond confused. Somewhere nearby a siren wailed. He lowered his voice. "I love you."

Teagan shook her head and smirked. He must have called last night after she turned her phone off, somewhere in the middle of his bar crawl. Max and his friends prided themselves on knowing all the bars in Philly that didn't card. They went on these road trips once every month, crashing at Trey Duncan's brother's dorm suite at Temple to sleep it off. Max must have been seriously sloshed if he had called her after 11 P.M.—her absolute latest bedtime if she wanted to get her proper beauty sleep. Plus he had called her "Sweet Bottom," which was so not her nickname. Max knew she hated anything that called attention to what she considered her massive posterior.

But she could forgive him since he said he loved her. He barely ever said that. And never in front of his friends.

Teagan dropped the phone and turned on the water in her marble shower full blast. She would have loved to have taken a soak in the Jacuzzi instead, with its ten high-powered jets and her new Philosophy Pina Colada bath bubbles, but there just wasn't time. She was going to need to get to the salon early if Michel was going to have time to work his magic. She looked in the mirror and grimaced. From the look of things, she should have been there an hour ago.

Interview with Teagan Phillips re:
Upcoming Sweet Sixteen Party
Transcript 1, cont'd.

Reporter: Melissa Bradshaw, Senior Editor,
Rosewood Prep *Sentinel*

MB: How many people are we expecting at this fabu party of yours?

TP: Oh, over three hundred.

MB: Will many Rosewood students attend?

TP: I'm inviting the entire sophomore, junior, and senior classes. Plus a few select freshmen. I'm sure everyone will show. Unless they *want* to miss the event of the season.

MB: Any friends from outside Rosewood?

TP: (*laughs*) Really, Melissa, who outside of Rosewood is worthy?

MB: I see your point. And how about family? Any family attending?

TP: (*back-of-the-throat grumble*) Only my father and his fiancée. And only because he's paying.

Chapter 2

Teagan froze when she saw her stepmother-to-be hunched at the kitchen counter, poring over the morning newspaper. The woman had her curly blond hair twisted into a poof ball on top of her head and was wearing some kind of muumuu garment. It was black and gold with red slashes all over it, like a jungle cat had ripped into the fabric and drawn blood. Obviously it was from a thrift store. She wore two clunky wooden bangles on one wrist and a hundred skinny gold ones on the other. The gold earrings she was sporting were bigger than her head. Well, at least bigger than her ears.

It took all of Teagan's willpower not to cut and run. But her morning smoothie was in the fridge. Unless she wanted her stomach rumbling all the way through her salon appointments, she wasn't going anywhere without her smoothie. Teagan stepped into the room and strode across the gleaming tile floor directly to the refrigerator.

"Teagan!" Karen exclaimed, her eyes wide with excitement. "Happy sweet sixteen!"

Karen swooped over and enveloped Teagan in a death grip of a hug, assaulting her nostrils with the scent of a thousand burned incense sticks. All Karen's pointy bones jabbed into Teagan at odd places, reminding her of just how skinny the woman was. What was a perfect size zero doing wearing a king-size bedsheet anyway? Didn't she know how lucky she was?

"Thanks," Teagan said grudgingly, trying to breathe. "And ow."

"Oh! Sorry! I guess I'm just excited for you," Karen said, releasing her.

The second Teagan was free, she yanked open the door of the state-of-the-art Sub-Zero and grabbed the travel cup full of protein smoothie. At least she could always count on Natsui to have her shakes and smoothies made and ready to go. Drinking the smoothie tasted like licking a tractor tire, but with zero carbs, minor calories, and lots of protein and fiber to fill her up, it was worth it. Sort of.

"Oh, you don't want to drink that," Karen said, taking the cup out of Teagan's hands. She grabbed Teagan by the shoulders and steered her into the dining room. Teagan thought about struggling, but the woman was freakishly strong. One of these days she was going to have to ask Karen about her workout regimen—maybe if and when Teagan stopped resenting her very existence. Like that was ever going to happen.

"Look!" Karen announced. "I made us breakfast! You like?"

Teagan's stomach gave a loud grumble as she took in the incredible spread before her. Karen laughed. Teagan wanted to die.

God, stomach! Have a little decorum! she thought, flushing.

"Sounds like you like!" Karen said, delighted. She flitted into the room and started making up a plate. Teagan could hardly believe her eyes. She hadn't seen this much food in her house since her father's last client dinner party three years ago. The calorie counter in her brain instantly whirred to life, adding up the colossal numbers. Laid out on the hand-carved, Italian-imported table for twelve was a huge array of pancakes (140 calories each), muffins (240 blueberry, 220 banana, and, oh dear God, were those chocolate chips?), breakfast meats (35 calories per bacon slice. She didn't even want to think about the sausage), and juices (hello, carbs!). Watching Karen pile it all up on the Lenox china made Teagan want to boot. Inside her mind, a digital readout tallied up what Karen was about to consume, scrolling higher and higher.

"Come on in! Sit!" Karen said, pulling out a high-backed chair.

Teagan wanted to scream. Didn't the woman see how huge Teagan was? What was she trying to do, prep her for fat camp? Get her out of the house for the summer so she could redecorate in the crappy Pier-One-meets-National Geographic style she seemed to love so much?

She better not be wearing that outfit to my party tonight, Teagan thought, watching Karen fold up the excess of cloth underneath her tiny frame. *Doesn't she realize a photographer from the Who's Who? page is going to be there?*

When Teagan didn't take her up on her offer, Karen sighed and looked at her all doe-eyed. "You should try to eat a real meal," she said, growing serious. "Your father worries about you."

Teagan raised her eyebrows and leaned one shoulder against the door jamb, crossing her arms over her chest. Her large Natalia crocodile hobo bag bumped against her hip. "Oh yeah? And where is my dad this morning, exactly?" she asked.

This should be good.

"You know he had an important meeting with the developers this morning," Karen said, slathering butter—*real* butter—onto a blueberry muffin. "He's working on that low-income-housing project."

Absent as always, Teagan thought, feeling numb. *Happy birthday to me.*

"Riiiight," Teagan said, gliding past Karen's chair and lifting her smoothie cup from the corner of the table where Karen had left it. She popped the top and took a sip. "Sounds lucrative," she said with an eye roll. "You know, it's interesting. Before he met you, he was building high-rise hotels and raking in millions. Now it's homes for the homeless."

Karen placed her butter knife down with a clang and Teagan smirked behind her cup. Was Saint Karen going to get all worked up? Maybe a feather would fall off her angel wings.

"Your father has come to a point in his life where he's able to reevaluate his priorities," Karen said patiently. "He's decided that he would like to give something back to the society that has been so kind and generous to him." She turned and looked pointedly at Teagan. "I'd think you would be proud of him."

"Oh, of course," Teagan said, leaning back against the sideboard. She reached over and toyed with one of the fresh lilies in the arrangement that was delivered each day. One of many that were scattered throughout the house.

Teagan *would* have been proud of her father's charity if he had started up a project like this all those years ago when her actual mother had suggested it. Or even after her mom had died—if he had started some kind of foundation in her honor. But no. He had just gone on making money hand over fist, catering to the vacationing "needs" of the wealthiest one percent and jetting off on business trip after business trip, leaving Teagan alone on every conceivable holiday known to man. Not once had he expressed any kind of interest in slowing down and taking on more modest projects. That was, until Karen had come along, clutching her philanthropy awards. Dear old Dad had snapped to when Karen had suggested he take a long, hard look at his life. Now suddenly he was Mr. Habitat for Humanity or whatever. Puh-*leeze*.

"He left you a gift," Karen said, pointing toward the far end of the table with the buttered end of her knife.

Much to her chagrin, Teagan's heart skipped an excited beat when she spied the small, glossy red box and white card near the edge of the table, next to a stack of colorful envelopes. She quelled the stirring immediately. Whatever it was, her father had undoubtedly commissioned his assistant, Kevin, to pick it out like he always did. And while Kevin had exquisite taste, opening gifts from him always left a bittersweet taste in her mouth. Well, mostly bitter.

Teagan walked over, picked up the box, and dropped it unceremoniously into her bag. She saw Karen avert her eyes as she did it and was happy the step-whatever had seen. Let it get back to her father. It wasn't like he was going to care anyway.

On top of the stack of cards was an orange envelope addressed to her in familiar handwriting. Teagan smiled slightly and tore into it, dropping the envelope on the table. Inside was a cheesy, bright yellow card shaped like a 16. The inscription inside read, *Hope your day is "sweet"!* Underneath, her old friend Emily had written, *Dear Teagan, Happy sweet sixteen, birthmate! Hope you have a fabulous day planned. Have some Cheetos and OJ and think of me! Love always, Emily.*

Teagan grinned, remembering the Cheetos-and-OJ day. When she and Emily were about eight years old, they had come home after a long day of school and playing in the park to find Emily's house dark and quiet. Her mother had left a note saying that she had to work an extra shift at the hospital and would be home in time for dinner. Starving from all the swinging and sliding, Teagan and Emily had raided the fridge and cabinets, but Emily's mom hadn't had time to shop in days.

"All I got is a bag of Cheetos. Crunchy," Emily said, crawling down off the countertop.

"And all I got is orange juice," Teagan said.

They looked at each other and stuck out their tongues, just imagining what the orange-on-orange concoction would taste like.

"Well, there's people in Africa who don't even have that!" Emily said, repeating one of her mother's favorite mantras.

"Okay, but if I get poisoned, it's your fault," Teagan replied.

They sat down at the kitchen table and laid out their snack. When Teagan washed down her first mouthful of chewed-up Cheetos with OJ, she thought she was going to puke. "Ugh! That's gross!"

"Ew! Mondo gross!" Emily agreed.

"It's grosser than gross!" Teagan laughed, grabbing another handful of Cheetos.

"Grosser than worm pies!" Emily put in.

"Grosser than worm pies with mucus icing!"

"Grosser than worm pies with mucus icing and ant sprinkles!"

And in this fashion they finished the entire bag and carton, laughing the whole way. Teagan chuckled now just thinking about it.

"Who's it from?" Karen asked.

"My old friend Emily," Teagan responded without thinking.

"What? What's funny?"

Suddenly Teagan felt caught and she frowned, stuck in a private moment with a person she definitely didn't want to be sharing private moments with. "You had to be there," she said, shoving the card into her bag.

Emily and Teagan shared the same birth date. Back when they were little, their parents threw a joint party each year, inviting all the kids in their class. They would blow out the candles on one huge cake together and trade presents after everyone went home. (Teagan would hand over any tomboy-ish items to Emily and Emily would happily relinquish makeup sets, ballerina shoes, and the like.) They lost touch around the ninth grade, when Teagan had started at Rosewood Prep and Emily had continued on to the public high school. Still, every year, like clockwork, Teagan received a birthday card from Emily. It always made her feel nostalgic. Sometimes it even made her feel a little guilty. She never sent Emily anything. If she did that, then Emily might expect something— like for the friendship to start all over again. And really, Teagan didn't have the time for that. What did she and Emily have in common anymore? Aside from the birthday thing.

"Emily, huh? Yeah. Your father told me about her," Karen said. "Today is her birthday too, right?"

Teagan looked up, surprised. No way did her father remember Emily's existence. He barely even remembered Teagan's.

Luckily her cell phone beeped, saving her from having to formulate a response. Teagan whipped the tiny phone out of her purse. The little text message icon had appeared. Teagan hit the button and read:

Happy birthday, princess! Luv, Max

She rolled her eyes and shoved the phone back in her bag. What kind of boyfriend sent a text instead of calling on the morning of his girlfriend's birthday? He was probably still so hungover he could barely lift his head. Very attractive.

But at least this morning he had remembered her *actual* nickname.

"Well, I'm outta here," Teagan said. "I have to get to the salon."

She had used a lot more than the recommended dollop of Aesop Violet Leaf hair balm to get her mane into a reasonably sleek ponytail so she wouldn't be mistaken for some crazy off the street when she walked into Michel's. At this point she was practically salivating for the professional shampoo and scalp massage and a nice dose of warm cucumber conditioner and sealant. Any day was better with a fabulous head of hair. That had to apply even to a father-forsaken, guilt-ridden, motherless sweet sixteen. A rumble of thunder sounded outside as if to remind Teagan that it was still raining on her parade as well. Like she needed a reminder.

"Are you going to eat something before you go?" Karen asked.

Teagan opened her mouth to retort, but Karen looked so crestfallen and small, sitting there at the end of the huge, deserted table in her tent dress, that Teagan snapped it shut again. Another twist of guilt tightened her stomach and she sighed.

"Fine," she said, grabbing a mini-muffin and a piece of bacon. She wrapped the muffin in a linen napkin and tossed it in her bag, then took a bite out of the bacon. "Happy?"

Karen's smile was huge. Suddenly Teagan missed her mother with a new and disturbing ferocity.

"Later," she said, turning around before Karen had a chance to notice the change in her expression—the random tears filling her eyes.

"Have fun!" Karen called after her as she hurried through the living room and drawing room and into the foyer, her heeled Miu Miu boots clicking against the shining marble floor.

Teagan grabbed her cherry-colored limited-edition Betsey Johnson umbrella and her Ralph Lauren trench from the coat closet and slammed the door. By the time she had gotten herself all belted in and covered up and was outside, she had squelched the inner drama and was back to her normal, composed self. Controlling her tears was one of her prime talents. It had taken years to cultivate, but today she had it down to a science.

Hurrying under the carport, Teagan waited for her father's two Doberman pinschers, Rodney and Dangerfield, to come racing over to her as they always did. They barked and wagged and jumped around but never touched her, highly trained purebreds that they were.

"Good boys!" Teagan said in her baby voice, bending at the waist. "Now sit!"

They both sat down immediately at her feet. Teagan tore the piece of bacon she'd snagged from the table and tossed one half to each of them. They swallowed the morsels without letting the meat so much as pause on their tongues. She did the same with the muffin and whipped the rumpled napkin back into the foyer, where it fluttered to the floor. Natsui would find it and pick it up. That was what she was there for.

At the end of the steps on the circular drive Teagan's silver BMW Z4 Roadster waited for her—top up, of course—purring away like a kitten, gassed and ready to go. As she approached, Jonathan, her father's staff mechanic, pool guy, and all-around guy Friday, opened the door for her.

"Happy birthday, Miss Teagan," he said, flashing his Hollywood-worthy dimples.

"Thank you, Jonathan," Teagan said, gracing him with a smile as she slid onto the leather seat. Karen was one thing. For Jonathan and his butt-hugging chinos, she could muster a smile.

Interview with Teagan Phillips re:
Upcoming Sweet Sixteen Party
Transcript 1, cont'd.

Reporter: Melissa Bradshaw, Senior Editor,
Rosewood Prep Sentinel

MB: So, where will this end-all-be-all party take place?

TP: At the Upper Sheridan Country Club, of course. My father and I have been members there for years.

MB: Oh, I love that place! The golf course is outstanding! Have you ever seen the view from the sixteenth tee?

TP: I'm not into sports. Real women don't perspire.

MB: Oh, well, I wasn't there to play golf, if you know what I mean. (*snickers*) But there *was* sweat involved.

TP: Do tell.

MB: Sorry. That would be a story for another time. And without a tape recorder running. Now, there will be music, I assume?

TP: No. We're using the dance floor for pottery

lessons. (*pause*) Of course there will be music.

MB: Band or DJ?

TP: DJ. I've hired Shay Beckford, actually.

MB: *Reeeaallllly?* Rosewood's own fallen and resurrected angel?

TP: You sound surprised.

MB: I wasn't aware that he did private parties.

TP: Well, he doesn't, normally. But when I want the best, I get the best. You should know that about me, Missy.

MB: It's Melissa.

Chapter 3

"Oh my God! Learn to drive!" Teagan muttered as the light turned green up ahead and no one in front of her moved. Nothing but brake lights as far as the eye could see. She slammed on her horn to no avail. Her windshield wipers beat back and forth like they were in a panic, slapping the waves of rain aside. "Move!" Teagan willed the cars in front of her. "It's just a little water. If it bothers you so much, stay home!"

The downtown area of Upper Sheridan was one huge traffic jam as everyone attempted to run their regular weekend errands in the deluge. A woman walked out of Touch of Class dry cleaner, struggling as her plastic-wrapped clothes whipped in the wind and her umbrella turned inside out. Women hustled in and out of the apothecary, stashing their prescription bags and tubs of eighty-dollar moisturizer in their purses. Couldn't these people wait until Sunday to do these things and leave the streets and parking spaces open for those with *actual* needs? There was even the usual line outside Natalie's, the local breakfast nook. Hungry would-be brunchers huddled under the tiny awning, trying desperately to keep dry as they waited for an open table. Although this, Teagan could understand. Natalie's French toast was to die for.

At least that was how she remembered it. She hadn't had any since the eighth grade.

Teagan could not wait to get to Michel's and kick back in one of those leather massage chairs. Her best friend, Lindsee Hunt, was meeting her there and had probably already ordered up a couple of skim lattes from the café counter at the front of the spa. Teagan practically salivated just thinking about it. This day was already making her into a total stress case and it had barely even started.

Outside her window, a man and his son ran for their parked Mercedes, ducked together under a newspaper. They were soaked through by the time they got inside their car. Finally! A space!

Teagan glanced in her rearview mirror. A Land Rover was coming up pretty quickly, but he was just going to have to stop. She put the car in reverse and backed up to let the guy and his kid out. The Land Rover slammed on its brakes and swerved, narrowly missing Teagan's back bumper. In her rearview mirror she could see the middle-aged man behind the wheel gesticulating wildly. Teagan simply shrugged. You had to do what you had to do.

She waited for the father to pull his Mercedes out into traffic. The Land Rover slammed on his gas and lurched around her, the midlife-crisis-having loser behind the wheel lowering his passenger side window to shout epithets in her direction. Unfortunately for him, it was a lost cause. Teagan could hear nothing over the sound of the rain pounding against her rag-top and the top-forty station blasting through her speakers.

Once the coast was clear, she pulled up alongside the front car. If there was one thing Teagan hated about driving, it was parallel parking. It always gave her the sweats—impatient people trying to get by her on the street, old fogies in the diner window, watching her technique. It was far too stressful. One of these days she was going to have to find a salon that provided an actual parking lot for their customers. Unfortunately, if a shopkeeper wanted the prime real estate on Sheridan Avenue, where all the hippest boutiques and jewelry stores were housed, a parking lot was pretty much out of the question. And besides, Michel had been cutting her hair since she was ten. He had identified all her cowlicks. He was aware of exactly how the layers should fall to disguise her awful pointed chin. Teagan knew she would never give him up.

Taking a deep breath, she cut the wheel and backed into the space. She cursed as she smacked into the car behind her. The dorks in the diner were laughing at her. Gripping the wheel, she cut it again and lurched awkwardly forward. Smack! The car in front got it too.

"Dammit," Teagan said under her breath.

She straightened the wheel and backed up a couple of inches, then put it in park. Deep breath. She was reasonably close to the curb. And Jonathan would buff out any scratches as soon as she got home. No harm, no foul.

Her cell phone trilled. Teagan glanced at the caller ID. It was her friend Ashley Harrison. She sighed and rolled her eyes. Ashley could keep a person on the phone for *hours*, but what was she going to do, ignore a birthday call?

"Hey, Ash," she said into the phone.

"Happy birthday to you! Happy birthday to you!" Ashley sang. "Happy *birth*day, dear—"

Teagan winced. Talk about off-key.

"Ashley, I hate to interrupt your unique vocal styling," she said sarcastically, jamming open the door of the car, "but I'm late for Michel's. Gotta go. See you tonight!"

"Oh, okay, well—"

Teagan silenced her by hitting the end button. Then she double-thought it and turned the phone off entirely before tossing it back in her bag. The last thing she wanted was to be interrupted while she was trying to relax at the salon. She raised her umbrella and carefully stepped out onto the street, trying to keep her coat and boots from getting wet. It was pointless, of course. Before she even got the door closed, the cuffs of her sleeves and the hems of her jeans were soaked.

"Why today?" Teagan muttered, fumbling to get her bag's strap on her shoulder. "Why do these things always happen to *me*?"

She slid between her front bumper and the other car, barely noticing the dent she had put in its fender, and stepped up onto the sidewalk, bypassing the parking meter that was flashing for her change. Let them give her a ticket. Having her father's accountant pay it would be a lot easier than fishing for her wallet in her monster bag while trying to keep the umbrella over her head.

Teagan squinted through the rain. Up ahead there was some kind of commotion on the corner. The corner she had to walk around to get to Michel's. She spied a yellow-and-white-striped awning and a banner draped across the arch-shaped doors of the neighborhood church. A few people in highly unflattering ponchos milled about, talking to sopping-wet pedestrians. She saw a woman lift a bag full of old clothes out of her car and hand it over. An elderly gentleman slipped a few bills into a bucket one of the poncho guys was proffering.

Oh, great, Teagan thought, quickening her steps. *Panhandlers.*

Just what she needed. She turned her back to the clutch of people as she breezed by, pretending not to notice that anything out of the ordinary was going on. No one stepped in front of her; no one called out to her. She was almost to the corner and it looked like she was home free. Maybe the birthday gods were finally starting to smile down on her.

"Teagan Phillips!" Some guy said her name in that way guys do. Like he was sizing her up even though he already knew who she was.

Teagan stopped in her tracks, cursed under her breath, and turned around, flipping her ponytail over her shoulder. Stepping out from under the awning, wearing a tatty, wrinkled poncho that just about covered his knobby knees but certainly not his hairy, cargo-shorts-sporting legs was none other than Shay Beckford. His work boots were darkened from the rain and his white socks were soaked through. Water dripped from the edge of his hood and his dark curls were plastered to his forehead, yet his smile was as wide as could be. Teagan sighed. What was a guy like Shay doing begging for money on a Saturday morning? It was such a waste of varsity soccer, honors student, equestrian champ hottie.

Not that Teagan thought he was all that, but it had been the general consensus at Rosewood Prep. He had won almost every class title in his senior yearbook. What a joke.

"Shay Beckford," she addressed him, tilting her head. "What are you doing here? Giving your parents yet another reason to sob over your baby pictures, wondering where it all went wrong?"

"Sharp tongue you got there, Teagan," he said, blue eyes twinkling. "You slay me."

"Shouldn't you be working on my set list right about now?" she asked. It never hurt to remind the help who was boss, especially when just trying to hold up her end of the conversation made her pulse pound annoyingly in her ears. Somehow she always felt like Shay was looking right through her instead of at her. Almost like he could see that her brain was reeling to think of comebacks even though she was keeping up a perfectly calm exterior. It was unnerving.

"Don't worry about your precious little party," Shay said. "I already dropped off all my equipment this morning and your set list is good to go."

"Good," Teagan said with a nod. "Wouldn't want any reason not to recommend you to all my friends."

"No offense, but I think this is my last teenybopper bash," Shay said with a grin.

Teagan narrowed her eyes. What was it about him that was so infuriating? The ego? No. She usually liked a little cockiness on her guys. The gorgeousness? No. She could look at him all day if he would just shut up. The fact that he had succeeded even though everyone had pegged him to be a big fat failure? Yeah, that could be it.

Shay Beckford had graduated first in his class from Rosewood Prep last year and had been handed his pick of Ivy League schools. But instead of heading off to Stanford or Harvard or Yale, he had shocked the entire Upper Sheridan community by taking the trust fund his grandparents had left him and renting a loft apartment in Manayunk, the up-and-coming artist neighborhood on the outskirts of Philly. Then, instead of blowing his bank on drugs, babes, and alcohol like everyone expected, Shay had bought all new DJ'ing equipment (he had dabbled in high school) and used the connections made on his many infamous party weekends to get a few gigs spinning weeknights at some of the hottest clubs in the city. Gradually he had worked his way up to Saturday night headlining gigs and dangerously packed houses. There were rumors that clubs in New York had courted him, but he had turned them down. Ever the hometown boy, he decided to forgo dirty water dogs for cheese steaks and stuck around.

Then last spring he had been hired by Mayor Reynolds—at a hefty price—to DJ at his daughter's spectacular, two-million-dollar wedding. Apparently young Chelsea, the socialite of the century, just *loved* Shay's work all those nights when she was slumming in the city with her friends. His performance at the wedding had won rave reviews, but Shay had refused to do private parties ever since, wanting to focus on his club career. (And not be labeled as "hired help," Teagan assumed.) Meanwhile he was always appearing in the press for some charity event or other, working for free to help various causes. According to all the press he had garnered, he was hanging with tons of local celebs and even a few national ones. He always looked so smug in the pictures. Just like he did right then, standing there in all his poncho'd glory.

When Teagan had decided to hire a DJ for her party, Shay had been the obvious choice. He had balked at first, citing his no-private-parties policy. But then Teagan had upped the price. And upped it. And upped it. Until Shay couldn't lucidly refuse. Teagan figured the money was well worth it—until he had been quoted in the *Inquirer* last week saying he was going to give the whole fee to charity. Like she *wanted* everyone to know she was throwing her money away.

But he *was* universally acknowledged to be the best in the Philadelphia area. And really, Teagan Phillips wasn't about to have anything less than the best. Of course, at that moment, staring him down in the rain, she was kind of wishing she had gone with the live band idea.

"Well, I should be going," Teagan said, hoping to make her escape before he made her feel stupid, as he always seemed able to do.

"Don't you want to make a donation?" Shay asked. "It's for the East Sheridan homeless shelter. We're collecting clothes, toys, appliances. . . ."

"Oh, and I always carry a dishwasher in my jacket pocket," Teagan said.

"And cash," Shay finished, eyeing her handbag. "Whaddaya got in that crocodile monstrosity of yours?"

Instinctively Teagan clutched her purse strap. She felt a blush creeping up her neck and into her cheeks. How irritating. If she didn't give him anything, he was going to think she was a spoiled brat and act all superior. If she did give him something, he was going to think he had some influence over her and act all superior anyway.

"Sorry, I can't help you," Teagan said with a forced smile. "My father takes care of all the family's charitable donations."

There. Argue with that.

Shay smirked. "Sweet sixteen and she still can't make her own decisions," he said. "Why am I not surprised?"

Teagan's mouth dropped open, but nothing came out. No matter. Shay didn't give her time to formulate a comeback anyway. He quickly turned his back on her and strolled over to the crowd, striking up a conversation with an elderly guy in a walker. Teagan's blush took over now, heating her every pore. God! Could Shay Beckford *be* more infuriating? He couldn't insult her and walk away. He couldn't insult her, period!

Except he just had. And she was still standing there in the rain like a moron.

Teagan turned to go, more than ready to vent her frustrations to Lindsee, and immediately a woman in a yellow raincoat stepped in front of her, holding one of those buckets. Teagan started to step around her, but then she saw her face and stopped in her tracks. The lady was completely bald, her eyes sunken and rimmed with purple bruises. She looked emaciated, yet she wore a positively radiant smile.

"Make a donation to the homeless, miss?" she asked. "Anything you can give will help."

Teagan swallowed a huge lump in her throat. This woman looked so much like her mother had the week before she died, it could have been her. For a split second, she felt her mom looking down on her and was overwhelmed by sadness and guilt.

She checked over her shoulder. Shay had been enveloped by the crowd. He wasn't watching.

"Hang on," Teagan said. She stuffed her hand into her coat pocket and her fingers closed around a bill. She barely looked at it before depositing it into the bucket. All she wanted to do was get the hell out of there.

"Fifty dollars!" the woman gasped. "Thank you, miss!"

"Yeah, no problem," Teagan muttered.

She was around the corner and out of sight before she could even think about looking back.

Rosewood Prep Sentinel

GOSSIP PAGE

Buzz, Buzz, Buzz
By Laura Wood, Senior Writer

With Teagan Phillips's sweet sixteen rapidly approaching, this school hasn't seen so much buzz since the legendary senior prank of 2001, when Lance Larsen let a hive of bees loose in the cafeteria. Here are just a few of the rumors running rampant through our halls.

"I heard she has an endorsement deal with Apple and she's giving out mini iPods as her favors." Free iPods? Who in this school doesn't already have an iPod?

"I heard Ryan Seacrest is gonna be there and he's gonna kick out one guest every thirty minutes." Seacrest is coming? There's one good reason *not* to attend.

"Instead of having bouncers, she hired WWE wrestlers to keep the freshmen out. Seriously. Those frosh better stay *miles* away." Poor freshmen.

"Dude, I heard she's having, like, supermodels there. Do you know if Giselle is coming 'cuz if she is, then I'm gonna hafta get a hair-cut." Note to the boys of Rosewood: Whether Giselle is going to be there or not is unconfirmed, but a new haircut is not going to get any of you in there.

"Apparently every girl who goes has to get her belly button pierced. I don't know about you, but I already have all the holes I need." That's either really clever or kind of gross, depending on how long you think about it.

"I overheard her yesterday talking about her big 'grand entrance'. She's going to be arriving by private jet! I'm serious! She kept talking about keeping the runway clear." Yeah, that's not a disaster just waiting to happen.

Well, there you have it, folks! The best of the best. So ladies, keep your hands over your tummies, and gents, don't provoke the nice wrestlers. Oh, and in case I can't make it, someone throw some birthday cake at Ryan Seacrest for me, will ya?

Chapter 4

"Happy birthday, girlfriend!" Lindsee greeted Teagan as she stepped into Michel's Salon and Day Spa. She held two champagne glasses full of bubbly orange liquid in the air. "I got us mimosas!"

Ah, mimosas. Far superior to skim lattes.

As always, Lindsee was the picture of perfection. Her long blond hair fell in gorgeous, gleaming waves over her shoulders. Her lip gloss shimmered and her brows were freshly waxed. She wore a scoop-neck, cream-colored Max Mara sweater over camel leather pants that hugged her ass like they had been slathered on with a butter knife. Nothing like a date with Lindsee to make Teagan feel like a frump. Still, she shook her ponytail back, lifted her chin, and smiled like a pro. It was all about attitude.

"Thank God—can you believe this weather?" Teagan asked as the salon staff rushed forward to whisk away her coat and umbrella without a word. Just the way Teagan liked her help—prompt and mute.

"I know," Lindsee said, handing Teagan her glass. "But don't worry. A little rain cannot bring Teagan Phillips down. Today is *your* day. And it's totally going to kick ass."

"You're right. I just need a little pampering and I'll be good to go," Teagan said. She lifted her champagne flute toward Lindsee. "And a little of this won't hurt either."

"I hear that," Lindsee said. They clinked glasses and downed the sweet champagne-and-OJ drinks in one gulp.

Teagan glanced around at the bronze walls, asymmetrical mirrors, and gilded sinks. Michel revamped his salon every year to keep up with the latest trends in haute decor. The place was like a continual homage to the TLC network and all its home makeover shows. But Teagan liked this latest incarnation. Thanks to the dark brown leather chairs, the burnt orange marble stations, the dark gold, suede-finish walls, and the sleek, geometric mirrors, it was warm without being too cozy. Chic without falling back on black. She felt at home here. Probably because she was here every other week, sitting in some chair or another, getting something buffed, waxed, or highlighted. With each decorating overhaul, the employee uniform changed as well. Today the stylists, hair-removal technicians, manicurists, and masseuses were wearing head-to-toe black. Last year it had been white lab coats and gray pants. Next year Michel would probably outfit them all in red unitards.

"Is there anything else you ladies require before your appointments?" one of the assistants asked, appearing soundlessly at Teagan's side.

Teagan pulled out her Prada wallet and slipped out her platinum AmEx. "Just take this now so I don't have to think about it," she told the woman, handing over the plastic. "Put everything on it and add the customary tip."

"Yes, miss," the woman said, scurrying away.

Lindsee grabbed Teagan's wallet out of her hand. "Omigod! What is this picture?"

Teagan looked over Lindsee's shoulder. Max gazed up at them in black and white, his light eyes smoldering. "Max got head shots done. He's gonna try modeling this summer."

"You're kidding me," Lindsee said. "I didn't know about this!"

"Why would you?" Teagan asked coolly, taking the wallet back. *He's* my *boyfriend*, she added silently.

Lindsey smirked. "Modeling, huh? That takes a special kind of cocky."

"Well, he *is* the hottest guy in school," Teagan replied, placing her empty champagne flute down on the nearest station.

"I don't know about *that*," Lindsee said, toying with her own empty flute.

"Oh, please! You totally wanted him last fall. You're just irritated that *I* got him," Teagan replied, laughing. This conversation was making her feel *much* better.

"I did not *want* him!" Lindsee protested.

"Yeah, you just keep telling yourself that." Teagan snorted.

Lindsee's jaw dropped and a squeak emitted from the back of her throat. "You know, if it wasn't your birthday, I could—"

"Ladies!"

Michel scurried out from one of the colorists' suites, his black shirt open all the way down to his navel, exposing an unnaturally hairless chest. Under the iridescent lights, the dark skin on his shaved head shone like a doorknob. His broad smile made his eyes squint so tight they were almost closed.

"There she is! The birthday girl!" Michel called out, kissing the air around Teagan's ears. "I must say, you do look older! You girls are blossoming before my eyes!"

Teagan blushed obligingly. Lindsee still looked a little annoyed, but she managed a smile.

"Now, Teagan, let's get you right to the sinks," Michel said, grabbing her arm and steering her up a few stairs toward the back. "With your hair and this weather, we have got our work cut out for us!"

Taking a deep breath, Teagan told herself it was time to relax. She was in good hands. Michel would take care of her. What would she do without him?

Teagan sat back in a cushy chair in front of one of the half dozen gold sinks. "Tamika is going to wash and condition you," Michel said with a smile. "Then we'll put on the sealant and you'll get your mani-pedis. After that, you're all mine," he said with an almost-lascivious grin.

"I can't wait," Teagan said.

Brooklyn, a gorgeous girl with butt-length red hair, approached with a smile. Teagan always wondered how Michel convinced all this eye candy to work as menial laborers.

"I hear it's your birthday," she said, her nose ring blinking under the soft lights. "Congrats."

"Yeah. She's touched. Where can we get some more mimosas?" Lindsee demanded curtly.

"You twenty-one?" Brooklyn asked, looking Lindsee up and down.

"You my mother?" Lindsee shot back. Teagan snorted a laugh. Brooklyn simply shrugged and blew out a breath.

"You'll have to talk to Sona at the café," she told Lindsee

with an air of perfect nonchalance. Teagan was impressed. Most people cowered or at least balked when they met Lindsee's snippy side.

Lindsee scoffed with impatience. "I'll be right back."

Teagan knew Lindsee was irritated about the Max conversation, but all she had done was tell the truth. It wasn't her fault if Lindsee was a sore loser. Plus if she knew anything about her cool-as-a-cucumber-mask best friend, Lindsee would be over it by the time she got back. Or at least she would pretend to be.

Brooklyn slipped a black coverall around Teagan's shoulders and clasped it behind her neck. She tipped Teagan's head back into the sink and Teagan rested her neck in the little cradling dip, closing her eyes. The water was warm and calming. Yes. This was good. Everything was good.

Teagan breathed in and out deliberately, trying to soothe away the last of her tension over the rain and her random morning encounters. With each breath she expelled another negative. Good-bye, Karen. Good-bye, bacon. Good-bye, idiot midlifer and his Land Rover. Good-bye, cancer lady. Good-bye, Shay. Especially, definitely good-bye, Shay.

"So, ready for the scandal of the day?" Lindsee asked, returning with the drinks. Clearly Max had been set aside.

"Absolutely," Teagan said.

"Maya and Ashley bought the same dress for your party," Lindsee announced, clinking the two glasses together in mini-celebration over this news. "I'm talking the same *exact* dress."

"You're kidding me," Teagan said with a smirk. That sounded like something her friends Maya and Ashley might do. They rarely thought for themselves and when they tried, they almost always came to the same conclusion. It was like after sixteen years of being best friends, they had actively dulled the personality right out of each other.

"Yeah, so Maya, like, freaked out, saying it was so much better for her coloring and Ashley lost her shit all over Maya for being so vain all the time and now they're not speaking," Lindsee said, snorting a laugh. "So pathetic."

"They're not speaking?" Teagan asked, her shoulder muscles coiling. "Great! Now I'm going to have to spend my entire pre-party listening to them bitch about each other."

"Don't worry, I'm *sure* it'll blow over by then," Lindsee assured her. "They're both out shopping for new dresses right now."

"Omigod, Ashley just called me to sing 'Happy Birthday,'" Teagan said. "She probably shattered the eardrums of every-one in Bloomingdale's."

Lindsee laughed.

"Wait. Why isn't just *one* of them shopping for a new dress?" Brooklyn asked.

"I'm sorry, were we talking to you?" Lindsee snapped.

Teagan opened her eyes and caught Brooklyn's look of instant ire, then watched her control it and go about her busi-ness. She knew better than to snap back at Lindsee. If she did, she'd probably be fired. Of course now she was ripping her fin-gers through Teagan's hair like she was trying to bald her.

"Neither of them wants the other's sloppy seconds," Teagan told Brooklyn, if only to her to chill out before she was scalped.

Brooklyn widened her eyes and blew out her lips like, *"That's some world you live in."*

Like you wouldn't kill to be where I am, Teagan thought.

After getting conditioned and having the sealant worked through her hair, Teagan was feeling decidedly more relaxed. The second mimosa went a long way toward helping the situation as well. Soon she found herself in that massage chair she had been daydreaming about, bumping around as the mechanism worked the kinks out of her shoulders and back. Her feet soaked in a warm bubble bath full of peppermint salt as one of Michel's manicurists buffed away at her fingernails.

"You'll never believe who I bumped into out on the street with the homeless people," Teagan said to Lindsee, who was getting shaped and polished in the next chair. Lindsee raised her perfect eyebrows. "Shay Beckford," Teagan said.

"Omigod. Why am I not surprised?" Lindsee replied. "Is he *homeless* now?"

"No. He was just helping them raise money," Teagan said.

"You mean helping them beg for cash so they won't have to get off their lazy asses and get a job," Lindsee said with a laugh. "I can't believe he's DJ'ing your party."

"Well, he *is* the best," Teagan said, trying not to squirm as the woman working on her hands tugged at her cuticles. If there was one beauty regimen Teagan could never keep up, it was her nails and cuticle beds. Twenty-four hours after every manicure, they were destroyed again. She just couldn't get herself to stop picking at them.

"Mother says if I have a sweet sixteen party, she'll call in a favor and get Coldplay to perform," Lindsee said, rolling her eyes.

"You didn't cave, did you?" Teagan asked, sitting up a little straighter. If there was anyone in Upper Sheridan capable of out-doing her on a sheer extravagance scale, it was Lindsee Hunt. Her parents were not only hugely successful cardio-surgeons but were rolling in old-family money. Plus they had worked their bypass magic on several entertainment bigwigs and were always being invited to Manhattan or out to the Hamptons for swank parties that appeared in *In Style* and *New York* magazine. The only reason Teagan had even attempted to throw the party of the century was because Lindsee had sworn she didn't want one. Therefore, Teagan was sure she couldn't be outdone.

"Please. No," Lindsee said, as if the idea of a huge bash in her honor was repugnant to her. "It was just her latest attempt at bribery. She wants to throw me a party so she can invite all her stuck-up friends and have an excuse to get drunk on Taittinger's and eat caviar all night. No, thank you."

"So we're still going to Cabo?" Teagan asked, relieved.

"*Bien sûr*," Lindsee said. "I just talked to the travel agent yesterday. All I want for my sweet sixteen is to be lying on a beach with my best friend getting a massage from some hot guy named Miguel."

"Sounds like heaven." Teagan sighed, leaning back again.

"So, are you getting anything good for your birthday?" Lindsee asked. "I mean aside from the sweet ride your father bought you."

"My father had almost nothing to do with that," Teagan reminded her. "He left me the brochures from the three companies he decided I could choose from and I went shopping with Jonathan."

"A gift in and of itself," Lindsee said. "Remember that time we caught him changing in the pool room?"

Teagan blushed. Jonathan's had been the first live-and-in-3D male anatomy she had ever seen. "How could I forget?"

"I dreamt about that for *months*," Lindsee said.

"Seriously," Teagan said.

"Anyway, speaking of gifts, what do you think *Max* is getting you?" Lindsee asked, raising her eyebrows. "Something . . . sparkly, perhaps?"

"I just hope it's not a gag gift like last year," Teagan said. "I mean, who does huge teddy bears anymore? It's so seventh grade."

"Well, if I had a boyfriend, I'd definitely want him to get me something sparkly," Lindsee said, absently toying with her gold necklace.

"Don't worry, Lins. I'm sure by the time your birthday rolls around, you'll have a man who'll buy you whatever you want," Teagan said, reveling again in the fact that she had a boyfriend and Lindsee did not. There weren't many facets of life in which she excelled over her gorgeous, stylish, smart best friend.

So sue me if I like to bring it up as much as possible, Teagan thought.

"I know I will," Lindsee shot back, a little snappish.

"Jeez. Defensive much?" Teagan asked.

Lindsee cast her a sidelong glance, then suddenly switched from bitter to boisterous. She turned in her chair slightly as soon as her manicurist finished her second hand. "Okay, but what do you *really* want for your birthday?"

Instantly Teagan's thoughts turned to her mother. She had a dim recollection of her sitting in a deep, cushy chair at some random birthday party of Teagan's when she was a kid. She remembered the way she had smelled when she pulled Teagan in for a hug. Like roses and cinnamon.

"Teagan? What're you thinking about?"

Teagan's heart skipped a startled beat. "Max."

Lindsee blinked, then her lips twisted into a knowing smirk. "Oh, *really?*" She lifted her mimosa to her lips and took a long swallow.

"Yeah, I'm thinking about having sex with him tonight," Teagan said nonchalantly.

Lindsee instantly spit out an entire mouthful of mimosa, showering the woman who was draining the tub at her feet. Flecks of champagne hit the mirror on the wall across from her and dotted the woman's arms and face. Teagan cracked up laughing.

"Ugh!" the woman shouted, then hurried out of the room.

Lindsee pressed her fingers delicately to her lips and coughed.

"Nice work," Teagan said.

Lindsee wiped her bottom lip with her fingertip, being careful not to smudge her nails. "Hang on. Are you *serious?*"

"Totally," Teagan said with a nod. "I'm thinking that once I'm done getting wasted at the open bar, I'll grab Max and take him back to one of those private suites at the club. You know how crazy I get when I drink."

"I do have a dim recollection of a little table dance incident at Maya's post-winter-formal party," Lindsee said, narrowing her eyes. "But won't your father freak?"

"Like he'll ever even know," Teagan said, taking another swig of her mimosa. Just thinking about her father made her bitter, and suddenly the bumping and grinding of the massage chair seemed positively medieval. She reached for the remote and shut it down. "Who needs this chair when I have Max to give me a full-body rubdown?" she said, adding a luxurious sigh for good measure.

Max—with his broad shoulders, his year-round tan (Teagan was the only one who knew he had an open account at LA Tans), that sideways smile he reserved just for her—had been dropping hints about his sexual needs for weeks. These hints grew less and less subtle by the day and Teagan figured that losing her virginity to him would be the perfect birthday present for both of them. If she could get up the guts to just do it already.

Lindsee downed the rest of her drink and grabbed the first passing employee to order another.

Teagan smirked at her reflection in the mirror. Her dark hair was slicked back behind her ears, just waiting for Michel's magical touch. Her brows had been plucked into slim arches and her skin shone from the deep-pore-cleansing mask, highlighting her high cheekbones. For the moment she was makeup free, but her green eyes shone as she pondered a night of passion with Max. Thinking about him was a lot better than ruminating about the party or her father or her birthday without her mom. Instead she focused on the mental movie of last Friday night, when Max had come over for a little one-on-one and he and Teagan had come closer than ever to doing the deed.

Teagan's father, as always, was off on a business weekend in San Francisco, (with Karen, of course) so there was no one to ask questions when Teagan suggested she and Max head up to her room. She had been thinking about surprising him with a condom and an invitation, but at the last minute she had chickened out. Max had insisted they leave the lights on and Teagan had panicked about how her fully naked body might look to her *FHM*-obsessed boyfriend. Instead Teagan had made sure most of the action stayed above the clothes, but by the time Max had finally pulled himself away, every single part of her anatomy had been pounding, aching for more.

So maybe tonight, if she didn't eat a morsel of food—which she wasn't planning on doing anyway in order to look hot in her custom-made Vera Wang—and if she kept the lights dim, maybe tonight would be the night.

"Teagan Phillips, you are so *bad*," Lindsee said with a grin.

Teagan gulped down the rest of her drink. "Was there ever any doubt?"

Interview with Teagan Phillips re:
Upcoming Sweet Sixteen Party
Transcript 1, cont'd.

Reporter: Melissa Bradshaw, Senior Editor,
Rosewood Prep *Sentinel*

MB: What about makeup? Will you be doing your own?

TP: (*laughs*) Missy, please! This is the most important night of my life! Sophia Killen and I have been working all year to perfect my color palette. She designed a line of cosmetics especially for me and is coming to my house to personally apply my face.

MB: It's *Melissa*.

TP: Right. Sorry. You just seem like a Missy. No offense.

MB: None taken. (*clears throat*) And Sophia Killen is . . . ?

TP: Omigosh! Only one of the biggest up-and-coming makeup artists in all of New York. She apprenticed at Bobbi Brown for years! Now she's breaking off to form her own company. I hear she's even stealing some of Bobbi's most important clients.

MB: I see. So there were no makeup artists in

the greater Philadelphia area who were up to snuff?

TP: Everyone knows that all the best people in fashion and beauty are in New York. If not, then LA, Paris, or Milan.

MB: (*audible sigh*) Okay, now that we've imparted that piece of highly valuable information, what about your boyfriend? I believe you're dating . . . (*sound of papers rustling*) Max Modell?

TP: I think everyone is aware that Max and I have been a couple since last year's Spring Fest.

MB: Will Max be escorting you to the party?

TP: Of course he will. I've already picked out his tuxedo. It's the sleekest little Hugo Boss. It was *made* for him. Literally.

MB: (*pause*) You had your boyfriend's outfit *made* for him?

TP: A girl has to make sure her accessories are impeccable. They are the first thing people notice, after all.

MB: Could you excuse me for a moment? I think I just tasted bile. (*sound of fumbling*)

END OF TAPE 1

Chapter 5

"Have all the flowers been delivered?" Teagan barked into her cell phone as she checked her reflection in the full-length mirror inside her walk-in closet. "Yes, miss," George Lowell answered in his ever-placid tone. As the manager of the most prestigious country club in the area, he always maintained his composure. Emotions were far too crass for a man in his position.

"And what about the stages? Have they all been set up?"

"The carpenters put their finishing touches on the runway a few hours ago, miss."

"And the drapes?"

"Draped."

"The velvet ropes?"

"In place."

"The wind machine?"

"Blowing like a hurricane."

"Well, I don't *want* a hurricane," Teagan snapped. "I want

an evening breeze on the beach. That thing messes up my hair and it's your head."

"Yes, miss. I'll tell the technicians to subdue the wind machine," George Lowell said.

"And what about the—"

"Everything is in order, miss. I would stake my reputation on it."

"It better be," Teagan said. "I've worked my ass off on this thing."

"I'm sure you have, miss."

If only that were literally *true*, Teagan thought, turning to the side and scrutinizing her backside. Although she had to admit that her custom-made Vera Wang did a great job of masking her humongous butt cheeks. It should have. The price tag had been ginormous. Teagan smoothed down the slippery light blue material, and the asymmetrical hem swished around her thighs and knees, tickling her skin. She had chosen the color as a homage to her mother, who was heavy into astrology. She had once told Teagan that the signature color of her birth sign, Taurus, was pale blue. Her mom dressed her in it almost every day as a kid and she had to admit, it was really quite becoming. She could totally see Keira Knightly wearing this exact dress to a premiere. But wait, did her arms look fat from this angle? Ugh! She was going to have to remember not to let anyone important see her from the side.

"Now, Miss Phillips, if I might ask . . . Is it absolutely necessary that I wear this . . . *ensemble* you've chosen for me?" George asked.

Teagan heaved a sigh. "What's the problem?"

"It's just a tad formfitting for my taste," he replied.

Teagan glanced at the clock on the wall of her closet. It

was already 7 P.M. She couldn't believe he was bringing this up *now*. She had sent him the black Dolce turtleneck and pants last week. If he had a problem looking chic and stylish instead of frumpy as he usually did in his tux and tails, he should have told her then.

"Well, let me ask you this, were you expecting a tip tonight?" Teagan asked.

"I . . . oh . . . well . . . it's customary for the special events manager to receive some sort of special compensation from clients, yes," George stammered.

"Then wear it with pride."

The doorbell rang and Teagan's heart did a twirl. Max was here. It was all starting. The biggest night of her life was about to begin.

"Gotta go, George," Teagan said into the phone. "Make sure your guys are out there with golf umbrellas when my limo arrives. I am not walking into this party looking like I just went down a log flume."

"Yes, miss. And might I take this opportunity to wish you happy bir—"

But Teagan had already hung up. She shook her hair back from her face, then fluffed it with both hands. The layers fell perfectly around her cheeks and chin, as smooth as silk. Michel really was a miracle worker.

"You look sensational and the party is going to be killer," she told herself. "This is going to be the best night of your life."

With a resolute nod to her reflection. Teagan turned and opened her bedroom door. Her breath was nearly taken away by the sight of Max standing there in his full tuxedo, holding a small silver box in both hands. His shaggy blond hair had been waxed and mussed to Brad Pittian perfection. His light hazel eyes betrayed not a hint of the hangover he must have spent all day fighting. His dimples were deep enough to swim in and his tight lacrosse-star bod had never worn anything so flattering.

"Hey there, princess," he said with a coy smile. "Happy birthday."

I am so going to have sex with you tonight, Teagan thought.

"What do you have there?" she asked, eyeing the gift as he stepped into her room.

"Just a little something for the most beautiful girl in the room," Max said, offering it to her with a slight bow. He really was in rare form.

"I'm the only girl in the room," she pointed out, taking the box.

Max blinked and stood up straight. "Good point."

Teagan ripped open the wrapping paper and fumbled with the black velvet box inside. When she finally got it open, she let out a little gasp. Sitting in the center of the box was a small open heart of tiny, sparkling diamonds. It hung on a delicate, almost invisible white gold chain.

"Max! It's beautiful," Teagan said.

He stepped closer to her. So close she could actually taste his recently applied cologne.

"You already have my heart, but I figured you might like one you could wear," he said in a husky voice.

"Nice one," Teagan joked. "How long did it take you to come up with that?"

Max's expression instantly changed. "God! Can't a guy get a little romantic anymore?"

"What? Come on! I'm just saying! It sounded like a line!" Teagan said.

Max shook his head at her and took the box out of her

hands. Teagan had the distinct feeling she had just spoiled a moment. But he couldn't have seriously thought that didn't sound like it had been pre-written. She was just messing with him. What was the big deal?

"Here. Let me put it on for you," he said flatly.

Teagan turned her back on Max and lifted her hair, knowing full well that if she was going to salvage the night with him, she was going to have to apologize. He could be such a big pouty baby sometimes. She straightened the necklace and checked it in the mirror.

"It's beautiful, really," she told Max, putting on her most syrupy voice. "I love it." Then she turned to him and slipped her arms around his neck. "And I love you too."

"Yeah?" he said, the smile returning.

"Yeah."

He leaned in and kissed her and Teagan let his tongue play with hers for exactly fifteen seconds before she tried to pull away. He held her firmly, though, and she finally had to almost push him off.

"Max! It took Sophia Killen half an hour to get these lips right," she said, whirling for the mirror again.

"Sorry, babe," he said, whacking her on the butt. "Let's go downstairs. The guys are gonna be here any minute."

Max turned and walked out and Teagan quickly touched up her lip liner and gloss the way Sophia had taught her. She grabbed her small silver handbag and her oversized everyday purse, which was stuffed with all the supplies she'd need to keep herself looking photo-worthy all night long. She touched the tiny heart and smiled. Maybe she should *tell* Max that she was planning on losing her virginity with him tonight. That would definitely keep him in a good mood.

The doorbell rang again.

"Babe! They're here!" Max shouted at the top of his lungs. Then she heard the telltale whooping, hollering, and hand slapping that came with every greeting of the boys as they arrived for photos.

Teagan sighed. Telling Max would just have to wait.

When she got to at the bottom of the stairs, she could already hear the boys in the living room, cracking open a bottle of champagne and laughing. She was about to join them when the bell rang again and she headed for the foyer instead. Mrs. Natsui was just opening the door for Maya and Ashley, both clad in slick black raincoats, struggling under the weight of two huge suitcases with large red bows attached.

"Happy birthday!" they trilled on seeing Teagan.

Ashley's blond hair was pulled back in a bun and the loose front pieces were stuck to her forehead from the rain. She dropped the suitcase she was carrying and rushed forward for a gleeful hug, but Teagan took a step back.

"You're soaked!" she cried.

"Oh. Right. Sorry," Ashley said, stopping in her tracks. "But check out your presents!"

Maya ditched her umbrella in the stand by the door and held up one piece of luggage, shaking back her short black hair. "It's the Louis Vuitton you wanted!" she announced.

"And . . ." Ashley bent and opened the bag she had brought in.

Teagan's jaw dropped. The bag was jam-packed with every one of her favorite products—Aesop hair balm, J.F. Lazartigue shampoo, Kiehl's lip balm and moisturizer, Bliss spa foot treatments, Chanel compacts, Bobbi Brown lip glosses, MAC eye shadow, and tons of other stuff.

"We spent *weeks* gathering up all this," Maya said. "Not that shopping is much of a chore for us," she added with a grin.

"Yeah, really," Ashley added.

"Wow, you guys," Teagan said, stepping forward. "This is so—"

Maya slipped off her coat and handed it to Mrs. Natsui. Ashley looked up and let out a gasp.

"What?" Teagan asked. "What's the matter?"

Ashley stood up and removed her own coat. "*This* is what's the matter!"

Teagan looked from one of her friends to the other and the color drained from her face. They were wearing the exact same green dress.

"You guys! Lindsee said you were going shopping!" Teagan wailed.

"I did!" they both said at the exact same time.

At that moment Lindsee strolled in without ringing the bell, lowering her umbrella. She took one look at the scene before her and cracked up laughing. Instantly Maya and Ashley launched into an argument. Teagan let out a groan, turned around, and stalked out of the room. Perfect. Now all anyone was going to talk about all night was Maya and Ashley's fashion faux pas and the two of them were going to be grumpy party poopers from here on out. Couldn't anything go right today?

"Why don't we get one of just the girls together?" Donnie the photographer suggested. He used his beefy hand to wave Max and his lacrosse buddies Marco Rosetti and Christian Alexi away from the fireplace.

More than happy to be released from standing straight in their penguin suits, the three guys grabbed one of several chilled bottles of champagne and slumped onto the couches around the parlor. Teagan stood arm to arm with Lindsee as Maya and Ashley gathered around them—Maya and Ashley, who were, as of now, definitely not talking to each other.

The green chiffon minidress in question had fluttery split sleeves and a gold, jewel-encrusted belt at the empire waist. It would have been pretty on, say, Rachel Bilson, but it made Ashley look pregnant and it made Maya look short. What either of them had been thinking, Teagan had no idea.

"I don't understand," Lindsee said through her smile as Donnie snapped away, creating hundreds of floating purple dots with his flash. "I thought you were both going shopping today."

"I did," Maya said, shooting Ashley an irritated look. It was then that Teagan noticed that Maya had worn a pair of green contacts over her normally brown eyes. Not only did they match the dress, they looked stunning against her coco brown skin. Girl knew how to accessorize. Maya's dad was African American and her mother was Latina. Thanks to her multicultural genes, Maya was pretty in an exotic, pixieish sort of way. Teagan often thought that if Maya had just gotten her father's height instead of her mom's petite frame, she would be in the running against Lindsee for best looking.

"So did I," Ashley added. She looked more put-together after having fixed her hair, but her brown lipstick and bronze blush were too dark for her porcelain skin. The girl had a round baby face and was constantly making the mistake of trying to look older by wearing too much makeup.

"Smile, everyone!" Donnie directed.

Ashley ran her tongue over her teeth and grinned. She had just gotten her braces off the week before and had developed the unsavory habit of testing the smoothness of her teeth every five seconds. It drove Teagan up the wall.

"Wait a minute. So are you trying to tell me that you both went shopping and you both bought *another* identical dress?" Teagan asked, turning to her friends.

"I like it," Marco said, letting out a burp. "It's like having twins."

"Hang on. Need to change the film," Donnie said, staring down into his camera as he turned away.

Teagan noticed Donnie's tuxedo shirt was pulling out from the hem of his pants, unable to make the stretch over his Santa-like belly. God. Couldn't Formal Photography have sent her someone she wouldn't have been embarrassed to have hovering all night? This had been the only little creak in her otherwise humming sweet sixteen machine. Trent Michaels, the world-famous fashion photographer whom she had booked for the party, had canceled on her at the last minute because *Vogue* had given him an assignment in the Maldives. Where the hell were the Maldives, anyway? Why did a place she had never heard of take precedence over the most important party of her life? Now she was stuck with Roly-Poly Man, who, once they got to the party, was probably going to eat half the food himself. Teagan grimaced as he bent over, exposing a hairy white back, and decided to focus on the fashion faux pas she *could* fix.

"Well, one of you has to go home and change," she said, turning to her friends.

"Yeah. You can't spend this whole night with your bitch

faces on," added Lindsee, who looked perfectly Grace Kelly in a silver beaded body-hugging sheath. "This is *Teagan's* night. Everyone has to have fun."

Maya and Ashley looked at each other and sighed. "Fine. But who has to change?" Maya asked.

How about both of you? Teagan thought. "Well, maybe Ashley should. . . . ." After all, it was far better to look short than preggers.

"Omigod! You think I look fat, don't you?" Ashley blurted, her brown eyes welling with tears.

"No! Of course not," Teagan said, not wanting to make the situation any worse. The last thing she needed was to deal with a breakdown. "To be honest, it's really not that flattering on either of you."

The boys all cracked up laughing. Maya let out an offended wail.

"Fine! If that's the way you feel about it," Maya said, grabbing her purse. "Maybe we should both go."

"Maybe," Lindsee said with a shrug.

Now it was Ashley's turn to gasp. "I'm outta here."

"Me too," Maya said.

Together they both stalked out of the room, grabbing their umbrellas and jackets. It took a full minute for them to decide who was going to get to storm out first. In the end they opened both the double doors and walked out together into the darkness, their twin umbrellas opening in unison.

"Think they'll come to the party?" Teagan asked.

"Who cares?" Lindsee said, letting her shoulders slump, like she was just *so* exhausted by their antics. "At least *we'll* be there."

"True," Teagan said.

"Okay, why don't you two ladies get together?" Donnie suggested, happily oblivious to all the drama.

Teagan stepped up next to her best friend and they embraced, hugging tightly as they often did for pictures. They hammed it up for the camera, doing some model poses and throwing out some sexy pouts. All the while Teagan watched Max watching them and she could tell he was getting turned on. Just thinking about him getting turned on turned *her* on.

God, he was hot. Sometimes she still couldn't believe he was her boyfriend.

"I'm definitely going to do it tonight," Teagan whispered to Lindsee. "Tonight is the night Max and I have sex."

Lindsee stood up straight and they both stared across the room at Max as Donnie snapped away.

Poor guy had no idea what was going to hit him.

"Okay! That's it!" Donnie said finally. "We're done."

Max checked his watch. "We should get going, princess," he said, taking a swig right out of the champagne bottle. "Your chariot awaits."

As everyone grabbed their things in the foyer, their voices echoed off the high ceiling, giving Teagan the sensation that the party had already started. She slid her arms into the sleeves of her shimmery gunmetal Donna Karan evening coat and smiled. She could not wait to get to the country club and make her entrance. Everyone would be scrambling for photos, clamoring to talk to the birthday girl, asking her for dances. Her night in the spotlight was finally here.

As Max opened the door, the phone started to ring. Teagan let out a groan.

"That might be one of the vendors. They're always forget-ting to call my cell," Teagan said, hustling for the kitchen phone as fast as her stiletto-heeled Jimmy Choos would carry her. By the time she got there, the answering machine had already picked up.

"Teagan? It's your father."

Little late in the day for my birthday call, isn't it, Dad? Teagan thought, tensing up at the sound of his voice.

"Are you there? I've been trying your cell all day."

Teagan turned on her heel and strode back out of the room, closing her ears to whatever he had to say. Trying her cell all day? Yeah, right. Then why didn't she have any messages or missed calls? One of these days her father was going to have to realize that modern technology was making it a lot more difficult to be a liar.

"Gentlemen, I am officially hammered," Christian said, slumping back on the wide leather seat in the white Hummer stretch Teagan had commissioned. He leaned sideways into Lindsee, who did not look pleased. Christian's normally curly red hair had been slicked back from his face, which brought out his freckles and made him look even more like a grade-schooler than he already did.

"You can't get hammered off champagne, bro," Max told him, grabbing the bottle out of his hands. "What kind of lightweight are you?"

Christian leaned forward. "Lightweight this," he said. Then he let out the loudest, longest belch Teagan had ever heard.

Predictably, the guys all cracked up laughing. Marco leaned

forward to slap hands with Christian and slid off the seat, hitting the floor with a bump. Teagan rolled her eyes and looked out the window. Could these people be any more immature?

Raindrops slid down the tinted window and raced sideways toward the back of the stretch, pushed by the forward motion. Teagan picked at her nails and focused on one specific drop, watching it wend its way from the top corner of the window all the way to the opposite corner on the bottom. She couldn't believe that her father had waited until almost eight o'clock to call her on her birthday. Well, actually, she could. Part of her was surprised that he had bothered at all. He probably thought that leaving her that gift this morning was enough. Get Kevin to send her something and he wouldn't have to bother to call. Totally typical.

He probably wouldn't even show up to the party tonight. Clearly he couldn't give a crap that it was her birthday. Maybe he'd have Kevin send a clown instead. As clueless as her father was, he'd probably think that was appropriate.

As the boys initiated a belching contest around her, Teagan tried to stop thinking about her father and focused instead on the party. She imagined all the people already gathered at the country club, chatting and milling about, sipping their drinks. At that very moment all her friends and their families were admiring the flowers and crystal and china, marveling at Teagan's exquisite taste, at the expense that had clearly been put in. She knew they were talking about her imminent arrival, wondering what she would be wearing, rapt with anticipation. In less than ten minutes she would be making her grand entrance. The moment she had been waiting for all year was about to happen.

So why did Teagan feel oddly devoid of any emotion?

"You nervous?" Lindsee asked her, noticing the space-out.

"No. I know everything's going to be perfect," Teagan said.

"Better be or you'll sue their asses, right?" Lindsee said.

The car went over a bump and the guys all bounced dramatically out of their seats, laughing and falling all over each other. Lindsee and Teagan rolled their eyes. Sometimes it was next to impossible to distinguish one of these guys from the other.

"Oh, man!" Christian said, sitting up and wiping champagne off his face. "One of you ladies got a mirror?"

Lindsee dug in her bag and handed over a compact. Christian checked his reflection and smoothed back a wayward curl, then checked his reflection from every angle, raising one eyebrow, then the other.

"Why couldn't I have been born rich instead of good looking?" he said with a sigh. Then he grinned. "Wait a minute! I'm both!"

"Dude, you lifted that joke off my grandfather. Get a life," Max said, grabbing the compact back and handing it to Lindsee, who snorted a laugh.

"You're hanging out with Max's grandparents now?" Teagan asked, baffled.

"Maxwell Modell senior is a wise man, and I was honored to spend the day out on the links with him and Max last weekend," Christian said, adopting an uppity tone. "It is not my fault if his grandson and namesake does not appreciate his unique perspective."

"Unique? Yeah, right. The man still gets his rocks off playing pull my finger," Max said, huffing.

"Ew!" Teagan and Lindsee cried in unison.

"Alexi wants to be old before his time when the rest of society would kill to be like us," Marco said. "Go figure."

"Whatever, Maxwell," Christian said, ignoring Marco. "You'll be singing another tune when Max the First leaves his entire fortune to me."

Max responded by giving Christian a dead leg with his fist, and suddenly all three boys had launched into a wrestling match on the far side of the limo. Lindsee squealed and got out of the way, plopping down next to Teagan.

"Why do we hang out with these losers?" Lindsee asked lightly.

"'Cuz there's no one else?" Teagan suggested, only half kidding.

"Seriously. So. Nice ice," Lindsee said, glancing at Teagan's new necklace.

"Thanks."

Teagan fingered the little heart Max had given her and smiled as he extricated himself from his friends and popped open their third bottle of champagne. It was a beautiful gift but nothing compared to the gift she was going to be giving him later. Her empty stomach grew queasy at the thought. Was it good queasy or bad queasy? Teagan couldn't tell.

"Cheer up, princess!" Max said, planting a wet kiss half on her mouth, half on her chin. "It's your birthday!"

"You're right," Teagan said.

She grabbed the champagne bottle out of his hand and leaned forward in her seat to avoid dripping any on her dress. She took a long, awkward chug and swallowed. If she was going to get wasted enough to be buck-naked with Max later tonight, she was going to have to start now. Like, right now.

"Happy birthday to me!" she said, lifting the bottle.

Her friends all cheered as she took another slug.

Yep. The more wasted, the better.

Interview with Teagan Phillips re:
Upcoming Sweet Sixteen Party
Transcript 2

Reporter: Melissa Bradshaw, Senior Editor,
Rosewood Prep *Sentinel*

MB: Melissa Bradshaw here, back with Teagan
Phillips, hostess of what is sure to be one of
the most-talked-about sweet sixteen parties of
the year. Teagan, if we choose to cover your
party, would you consent to having a staff-
photographer-slash-reporter present?

TP: Who would it be?

MB: Well, probably me.

TP: Missy! Are you trying to snag yourself an
invite? Because as I already mentioned, the
entire senior class will be invited. Last time
I checked, that includes you.

MB: I'm not trying to snag an invite. I'm simply trying to secure your permission for on-
site coverage of the party so that we don't
have to rely on the badly lit digital candids
of your entourage, which, while they would
undoubtedly be very revealing, would probably
not be the best quality.

TP: Well, of course you can come to the party

and of course you can take as many pictures as you want.

MB: Gee, thanks.

TP: Are you feeling all right, Missy? You look a little red in the face. It's not very attractive, especially on a redhead like yourself. Girls like you really need to work harder to keep their emotions in check. It's doubly beneficial, actually. It will also help prevent premature age lines. And I saw your mom at the last school fund-raiser. You have some real genetic hurdles to overcome, you know? You should really start thinking about that.

MB: (*clears throat*) Thanks for your concern. Let's get back to the interview, shall we?

TP: Absolutely!

MB: Good. Now, will there be alcohol at this party?

TP: Of course! I've ordered several cases of Taittinger's because, well, as we all know, a party is not a party without a little bubbly. And there will also be an open bar stocking all the top-of-the-line brands. Only those over twenty-one will be served, obviously.

MB: Obviously. (*sound of mutual laughter*) And will there be a theme?

TP: Oh yes. This is the best part! It's going

to be High Fashion. I toyed with the idea of doing an India theme—you know, Buddha, *mendhi*, and all that. But then I thought, India is just so *over*, you know?

MB: Yeah, I'm sure the people of India would be pleased to hear that.

TP: Right?

MB: So, High Fashion is your theme. Meaning . . . ?

TP: Meaning all the waiters and waitresses will be dressed in black uniforms designed by Nicole Miller instead of those tacky polyester tuxedo things they normally wear. Plus I got them all Gucci sunglasses. They're going to look so chic! I've also hired a dozen models to circulate throughout the room wearing Teagan Phillips originals.

MB: Teagan Phillips originals?

TP: Yes. I'm a designer.

MB: Really?

TP: Yes! I can't believe you didn't know that! If you want to be a reporter, you really should pay more attention to your . . . what do they call it? Your beat!

MB: Right. And why should I have known you were a designer?

TP: I only won the Pennsylvania Textiles Association's Young Designers award last year.

MB: Oh. First place?

TP: Honorable mention.

MB: Ah.

TP: Anyway, I have worked my fingers to the bone getting these designs ready for the models to wear at the party.

MB: A lot of sewing, then?

TP: Oh no. I don't sew them myself. I gave the designs to the freshman home ec class. They've been working on them since Christmas. But let me tell you, wrangling a bunch of freshman girls is *not* an easy job. Would you believe that one of them doesn't even have a cell phone?

MB: No! Tell me more about the models. How did you find them?

TP: Well, that part was the hardest. All the girls that showed up for the first audition were these, like, six-foot-four stick figures. I couldn't have *that* walking around my party.

MB: Because . . . ?

TP: Because this is *my* night. Everyone should be watching *me*.

MB: So you hired ugly models.

TP: Now, that was the tricky task. I had to find girls who were *attractive* but not taller or thinner or prettier than myself. It took *weeks*.

MB: But you found them.

TP: I found them. (*sighs dramatically*) Finally.

MB: Well. Thank God for that.

Chapter 6

Four tuxedoed valets were waiting for the Hummer when it
pulled up the winding, flower-lined drive to the country club.
Teagan looked out the window at the rain-soaked grass and the
wilting petals and started picking at her fingernails. This was
not at all as she had pictured it. And she had pictured it many
times, every day, for the past twelve months.

"You ready for this?" Lindsee asked. The Hummer pulled
to a stop and one of the valets opened the door.

"You guys go in ahead," Teagan said. "I'm going to wait a
couple of minutes."

"Why?" Max asked. "Don't want to be seen with us?"

"Yeah, what are ya? The queen of England?" Christian
joked.

"Dude, seriously. Quit channeling the grandpa," Max
snapped at him.

Teagan's eyes flashed. How stupid were they? Did they
really think it was appropriate for the guest of honor to enter

the party in the middle of a crowd, unnoticed? Besides, she had only told them a million times about the grand entrance she had planned.

"It's my party," she snapped. "I'm walking in alone."

Max blew out a sigh. "Fine," he said, stepping out under one of the umbrellas.

"Lindsee! Here! Take this and put it in the bridal suite," Teagan said, shoving her large black bag at her friend. She had insisted that the club let her use the largest and most posh suite in the place. It was closest to the ballroom and had three couches, a three-way-mirror, and its own private bathroom.

"Got it," Lindsee said, taking the stuff. "Break a leg!"

Max offered Lindsee his hand as she stepped out of the limo and they crouched under an umbrella together, half jogging up the flagstone walk to the awning at the door. The other guys followed, Christian still clutching the neck of one of the champagne bottles. Teagan waited until they were inside, then started counting to one hundred.

One, one thousand, two, one thousand.

"You coming?" one of the valets asked. He was her age and probably went to one of the public high schools in the area.

"In a minute," she snapped. "You *could* close the door before I catch pneumonia."

The kid scoffed and slammed the door, shaking the entire vehicle. Teagan's jaw dropped. That kid was so fired.

Where was I? Right. Three, one thousand, four, one thousand.

Even though her heart was pounding with anticipation, Teagan diligently counted all the way up to one hundred. She knew that the longer she took, the more the whispers in the ballroom would mount. By the time she was done, she felt nauseated from all the butterflies. She wasn't used to feeling this nervous. But then again, she had never had a more important night in her life. Everything had to go perfectly. She would kill someone if it didn't.

Finally Teagan took a deep breath and rapped on the glass. The door opened again and she placed one strappy blue-and-silver Jimmy Choo on the asphalt, making sure she was balanced before stepping all the way out. The kid who was so fired closed the door behind her and escorted her up the pathway. Teagan had to pick her way across the flagstones, making sure her four-inch heel didn't sink into the soft, muddy spots between the slabs of rock. It was slow going, and by the time she got to the awning, she could feel a sheen of sweat forming on her skin.

"Have fun," the kid said sarcastically as he dropped her off at the awning.

Teagan shot him a withering look in return.

The doors opened for her and she walked into the drawing room.

"Good evening, Miss Phillips," one of the two doormen greeted her.

Teagan ignored him. She could hear the low rumble of voices coming from the ballroom on the other side of the double doors before her. The music played at a respectfully low volume and the clink of crystal and silver trays could be heard even through the doors. Teagan slipped out of her jacket and handed it to one of the doormen, letting the cool air-conditioned air wash over her. She shivered but was glad, at least, to feel the sweat on her arms dry right up.

"Miss Phillips! Happy birthday!" George Lowell opened the doors and slipped out, being careful not to let anyone see in or out of the room.

Teagan almost laughed when she saw him, then remembered that she herself had selected his outfit. The turtleneck top was, in fact, a little binding. She could see the outline of his pecs—not bad for an older guy—but also the roundness of his little belly. Not an attractive combo. As always, his gray mustache was clipped and his balding head gleamed as if it had been waxed. "You look beautiful tonight, Miss Phillips. If you'll come with me, we'll get you ready for your big debut."

He held out his arm and Teagan took it. Together they walked around the side of the ballroom. The room was octagonal in shape, with doors on each of three consecutive walls. While most of the guests had entered the ballroom through the first door, Teagan would be making her entrance through the door in the center.

"Thank you," Teagan answered. She held her hands behind her back to keep from messing with her nails.

"Shall I tell Mr. Beckford that you have arrived?"

"Why would you tell Shay?" Teagan snapped, her heart skipping a few thousand beats.

Lowell blinked in confusion. "He is to announce you, is he not?"

"Oh! Right!" Teagan said. *Duh.* "Yes. Please tell Mr. Beckford I'm here."

"Good. Right away, miss. Break a leg!"

The club manager slipped back to the first door. The murmur of voices inside the ballroom heightened with his entrance. The people milling around inside were no strangers to parties like these. They knew that Lowell's quick return meant the guest of honor's entrance was imminent. Teagan breathed in and out. It felt like an eternity passed before Shay finally picked up the microphone.

"Ladies and gentlemen, if I can have your attention, please," he said. His voice sent tingles all over Teagan's skin, but that was just because he was about to announce her. "It's the moment we've all been waiting for. . . ."

Was there a hint of sarcasm in his tone, or was it just her?

"Let's give it up for our hostess and Miss Sweet Sixteen herself, Teagan Phillips!"

This is it, Teagan thought. *Take it slow. Don't trip. Make sure you give the photographers plenty of time to get every good angle.*

The doors in front of her were flung open and Teagan stepped out onto her custom-made runway, striking a pose. The jam-packed room erupted in cheers so intense, she felt like Beyoncé taking the stage at the First Union Center. A bright white spotlight shone down, temporarily blinding her, but she knew from the sheer din that the turnout was legendary. Everyone was here to celebrate her.

As Teagan strutted down the runway, she concentrated on the walk she had practiced a thousand times. Chin up, hands slightly swinging, hips swaying back and forth. All around the catwalk, in roped-off areas, were professional photographers and a few of her select friends who had been granted permission to sneak in with their digital cameras. The number of flashbulbs popping rivaled the red carpet at the Oscars. She saw Missy from the school paper busily clicking away. A couple of older guys from the local papers had gotten prime real estate at the end of the catwalk. Roly-Poly Man himself was front and center.

Teagan's smile widened when her eyes adjusted and she saw the masses of people packed into the ballroom, shoulder to shoulder in their tuxes and gowns. So many pairs of admiring eyes trained on her. Women gushed to their husbands, clearly jealous of how perfect she looked in her Vera Wang. Max and Lindsee and some other friends from school stood in a crowd by the bar, hollering and applauding.

The room looked spectacular. Huge white flowers burst from marble pots placed all along the walls. The lilies on the tables were gorgeous and the light-blue-and-white place settings were exquisite. Votive candles were scattered all over the room, flickering merrily in the dimmed light, and aqua-and-gold place cards hung from the back of each chair by a slim blue ribbon—a little touch Teagan had picked up in *Martha Stewart Weddings*. The cards were written by hand by a professional calligrapher, of course, as were the menu cards on each table. A package of Amedei chocolates imported from Italy sat in the center of each gold-rimmed salad plate—favors that the guests would either gobble before the bananas foster and birthday cake were presented or would take home to savor later.

Waiters circulated the room with shrimp scampi, salmon en croute, lamb chops with wine sauce. The women wore black minis and black halter tops, while the men were sporting skintight black Lycra tees and black, flat-front slacks. They all wore the same black, pebbled Gucci sunglasses and everyone's hair was slicked back. For a bunch of blue-collar workers, they looked *très* chic.

Across the room, the floor-to-ceiling windows were draped with dozens of blue, green, and aqua swags—to match Teagan's dress, naturally—that tumbled gracefully to the floor and, in some cases, trailed out toward the tables. Set up along the windows were all the fashion experts Teagan had hired. A colorist sat behind a table filled with color wheels and clothing samples, there to help willing guests determine their season. A hairstylist with a high-tech digital camera and laptop would take pictures and work her technical magic to show people what they might look like with a different style or color. Two guys from a tattoo parlor downtown were ready and willing to apply temporary tats and—this was Teagan's favorite part—give free body piercings to anyone who wanted them, behind a white curtain, of course. Ricco Durazo, who was standing next to his station with a huge smirk on, had done Teagan's own belly button piercing last summer and it was one of Teagan's most deeply held beliefs that anyone with a flat tummy should have one. *Only* those with a flat tummy, of course.

But the pièce de résistance was the models. As Teagan struck her pose at the end of the runway, she could see them circulating around the room, looking gorgeous in her one-of-a-kind designs. At the corners of the dance floor small round stages were placed, where more models vogued for the guests.

Everything was just how Teagan imagined it. Not some stupid, childish party with fire eaters and a pig on a spit, but a night of pure elegance. Take that, Shari Marx. She was just about to start wallowing in her triumph when she realized she might have gloated too soon.

Because . . . wait a minute . . . who had spread silver confetti all over the white tablecloths? She hadn't ordered that. It was so gauche. And what was with all the twinkle lights strung from the ceiling? What was this, junior *prom*? And wait, no one was drinking champagne. She had expected hundreds of bubbling glasses to be lifted toward her as she arrived. Where was the Taittinger's? There was supposed to be a chilled bottle of Taittinger's at every table.

"Isn't she lovely, ladies and gentlemen?" Shay said.

The applause grew louder, but Teagan shot Shay a look of

death as she executed her final turn. There was no mistaking the sarcasm that time.

Finally Teagan's gaze fell on her father in his Geoffrey Beene tuxedo, waiting for her at the bottom of the stairs that led up to the catwalk. His dark hair had been recently cut and was perfectly styled. He looked, as always, James Bond handsome. For a split second Teagan was almost pleasantly surprised to see him there, but then she saw Karen. Karen, with her arm through Teagan's father's, politely applauding Teagan's arrival, watching her with proud eyes. Seeing the two of them standing there like they were her parents, like Karen was her *mother*, Teagan almost missed the first step down from the stage. Her stomach and heart lurched together as one, but she threw her arms out and saved herself before anyone but those closest to her even noticed.

Who does she think she is? Teagan thought, her blood starting to simmer.

Almost worse than the parental display was Karen's outfit. She was not, as Teagan had feared, wearing that awful muumuu from that morning. No. It was much worse. She was wearing a slinky black Armani dress that clung to her slim body in all the right places. Her hair was pulled back in a sleek chignon and diamond studs sparkled in her ears. She looked, in a word, gorgeous.

What the hell was up with *that*?

Okay, my stepmother-to-be is not supposed to look sexier than I do.

Teagan glanced at her father and instantly saw the look of disapproval on his face. He was staring at her like she was some huge disappointment. Oh God. She knew it! She looked fat in this dress! So much fatter than his perfect, lovely little fiancée. The second she got home, she was throwing out that stupid mirror in her room. It was too flattering. She needed to know how she *really* looked before she left the house.

I can't believe this is happening, Teagan thought as the applause died down. The glitter, the lights, the stick-figure step-mom-to-be. And—oh my God—was that cheesy Shari Marx over by the dance floor wearing the exact same Jimmy Choos Teagan had spent months shopping for? Her fingers curled into fists at her sides. *I can't believe* this *is my sweet sixteen.*

"Let's get this party started!" Shay shouted as Teagan stepped down onto the ballroom floor.

Unbelievable. She had hired him because he *wasn't* supposed to sound like a bat mitzvah DJ. Was he doing this just to piss her off? If so, it was working. As were plenty of other things.

Shay cranked up the volume, dropping a recent dance hit, and everyone cheered as the crowd broke up into little klatches, chatting and laughing. At least two dozen people rushed Teagan, smooching her cheeks and shouting, "Happy birthday!" and "You look gorgeous!" directly into her ears in order to be heard over the music. Teagan's eardrums tweaked and her temples throbbed. Envelopes were pressed into her hands and her nostrils were clogged with a hundred different perfumes and colognes. Someone's thick, over-sprayed hair whipped her in the face, and a particularly stiff organza flower on someone's dress scratched her upper arm. Teagan felt nauseated and didn't even try to smile. Through the mayhem she could see her friends already starting to burn up the dance floor. All Teagan felt like doing just then was burning this place down.

"Sweetheart! Happy birthday!" Teagan's father said when

the crowd finally dispersed enough for him to get to her. He managed to crack a smile as he pulled her into his strong arms. Teagan patted him back halfheartedly, concentrating instead on squelching the sudden, angry, and disappointed tears that flooded her eyes.

"Whatever, Dad," Teagan said, pulling away.

"What's the matter?" her father asked, his face creased with concern.

Teagan cast a sidelong glance at Karen. "Oh, *nothing*," she said pointedly. "I need a drink."

And I need to not see the stepmonster-to-be for the rest of the night, Teagan thought as she started for the bar at a fast clip. She skirted the dance floor, where Max, Lindsee, Marco, Christian, and some others were drunkenly busting an awkward move, and wove her way through the onlookers instead. At least most of them had the foresight to get out of her way. At that point, Teagan wouldn't have been above shoving a few people aside. All she wanted to do was put as much distance between herself and her "parents" as possible.

"Teagan! Happy birthday!" one of her father's faceless, personality-free colleagues called out, handing her an envelope as she passed by. She snatched it out of his hand and kept moving without so much as a backward glance.

"You look lovely, darling," Lindsee's mother told her, handing over another envelope.

Yeah, right, Teagan thought, glancing at Mrs. Hunt's lifted eyes and lipo'd ass. *Bet you can't wait to get back in the car tonight so you can rip me to shreds.*

She stepped on the train of some old lady's gown and tripped forward a few steps. Grabbing a chair in desperation, Teagan managed to right herself and cursed under her breath, her mind swimming. So much for not being able to get a buzz from champagne. But it wasn't enough to take the edge off what she was feeling now. She needed something stronger.

Finally Teagan arrived at the huge bar in the back corner of the room. She slapped her pile of envelopes down on the surface and the bartender snapped to attention.

"What can I get you?" he asked with a bright smile.

"Apple martini," Teagan said.

The bartender's smile widened. "I can get you an apple *juice.*"

"*What?*" Teagan snapped. She felt like she could lunge across the bar, grab the skinny dude by his lapels, and spin him.

"No alcohol tonight. Sorry, miss."

"Uh, no. I don't think so," Teagan said shrilly. "I ordered the full open bar for five hours. I even went over the stock list myself."

"Well, then someone changed the order," the bartender said with an infuriatingly blasé shrug. "I got nothing but soda, sparkling cider, juice, and water."

"*What the hell are you talking about!?*" Teagan screeched.

"Them's the rules," he said, clearly enjoying this.

Teagan crumpled a few envelopes in her fists. Her nostrils flared as she turned around, searching the room for George Lowell. Someone around here was going to pay for this. Someone was going to pay dearly.

Interview with Teagan Phillips re:
Upcoming Sweet Sixteen Party
Transcript 2, cont'd.

Reporter: Melissa Bradshaw, Senior Editor,
Rosewood Prep *Sentinel*

MB: You mentioned you were only inviting your father because he was paying. Does this mean that the two of you have a strained relationship?

TP: I didn't say that. When did I say that?

MB: It's right here in the transcript from our first interview. (*sounds of paper rustling*) Here it is. I asked you if you would have any family at the party and you said, and I quote, "Only my father and his fiancée. And only because he's paying."

TP: Well, you can't print that.

MB: Sorry, but it's already on the record.

TP: My father and I have a *fine* relationship. If you print that we don't, I'll sue your [edited for content] for libel.

MB: Do you even know what *libel* means?

TP: *Missy*, Are you condescending to *me*?

MB: You're kind of obsessed with appearances, aren't you?

TP: Excuse me?

MB: I mean, you're clearly lying to this reporter about how you feel about your father. Is it really that important to you that the readers of the *Sentinel* think your home life is so perfect?

TP: Who the hell do you think you are? We're supposed to be talking about my sweet sixteen, not my non-relationship with my father.

MB: So you admit it's a non-relationship.

TP: (*fumbling sounds*) That's it! This interview is over! And you can kiss your all-access pass good-bye! (*sound of door slamming*)

MB: That was kind of fun.

END OF TAPE 2

Chapter 7

Teagan saw her father bust out of the crowd, Karen tripping and wobbling along at his heels like a little lapdog. The woman might *look* beautiful, but she certainly didn't know how to maneuver in those Prada heels. Teagan narrowed her eyes at their approach. As much as she didn't want to see them at that moment, they were as good a pair of people to yell at as any.

"I don't *believe* these idiots!" Teagan shouted. "There's no alcohol!"

A middle-aged couple moved away from her, looking disturbed. Thanks to Shay's music and all the raucous conversation and laughter filling up the room, no one else heard her yell.

Her father reached out and placed his warm hands on her upper arms. His grip was firm, as if he was hoping to hold her there in case an earthquake hit. For a split second Teagan was actually grateful for his solid presence. At this point, between her anger, her buzz, and her empty stomach, the room *was* kind of spinning.

"I know, honey," her father said. "I called George Lowell this afternoon and canceled the open bar."

Teagan felt like her father had just hauled back and slapped her across the face. She could not have been more shocked.

"You did what!?!" she screeched.

This time at least a dozen people turned to see what the commotion was about. Each stunned face was another humiliation for Teagan.

This. Is not. Happening.

"I'm sorry, honey, but I just didn't think it was appropriate to have an open bar at a party in which the majority of the guests were underage," her father said. "I tried to call you all day to let you know, but your machine kept picking up."

Teagan's fingernails dug into her palms. Her vision swam. Her skin was so hot she felt like she had passed out on a tanning bed at Michel's without sunscreen. Teagan had thrown many fits over the years. She was the queen of tantrums. Every other day something made her so angry she could explode. But at that moment she knew that she had never felt *this* infuriated in her life.

"Who . . . the hell . . . do you think . . . you are?" she said through her teeth, glaring at her father.

Karen gasped. Her father went white. "Excuse me?"

"You heard me," Teagan practically growled. "I worked for *months* on this party. *Months!* And you swoop in from God knows where after I haven't even seen you for two weeks and you ruin everything in one afternoon. Do you have *any* idea what you've done to me? My entire school is here. Everyone is going to be laughing behind my back! They're going to think I'm a huge loser!"

It took her father a moment to recover himself. When he did, he was shaking. "Teagan, I am your father. How dare you speak to me that way!"

"How dare you call yourself my father!" Teagan replied, her eyes hot with unshed tears. She knew even as she said it that it was an evil thing to say, but at that moment she couldn't have cared less who knew. "If you were a real father, you could never have done this to me!"

With that, Teagan turned around and slammed right into a miniskirted waitress. The huge silver tray she was toting tilted and smacked Teagan right in the face. She felt something heavy and wet plop onto her chest and dribble, cold and gloopy, down her cleavage. Shrimp showered the hardwood floor around the bar.

"Omigod! I am *so* sorry!" someone said.

Teagan opened her eyes and saw red. Red cocktail sauce splattered all over the neckline of her one-of-a-kind Vera Wang. It dripped all down the front of her dress toward the hem and a huge glop plopped right onto her freshly mani-cured toe, settling on and around the straps of her ridiculously expensive Jimmy Choos. The thick mess slid between her breasts and down her stomach toward her La Perla thong.

Karen lunged toward Teagan with a pile of napkins from the bar. Teagan stumbled backward, away from Karen, glaring the klutzy waitress in the eye. There was something familiar about her. Like Teagan had seen her before in a movie or a photograph, but she was too pissed off to think about it.

"I'm so sorry," the woman said, tearing off her Gucci

sunglasses. "It's these stupid shades they made us wear! None of us can see anything with these on!"

Teagan quaked from head to toe. Not only did this woman just destroy her dress and mortify her in front of her guests, now she was telling her that she was stupid for asking the help to look semi-presentable? She was an *employee*, for God's sake.

"You are *so* fired!" Teagan growled.

Instantly George Lowell was at Teagan's side, clucking over her dress. "Oh, Miss Phillips! What a shame! I do apologize," he told her, shaking his head. "Come. We'll rush you back to the suite and see what we can do."

Teagan glanced around and saw a few of her acquaintances from Rosewood eyeing her in an amused way or placing their hands over their mouths in shock. Missy Whatever Her Name Was snapped pictures so quickly her flash was like a strobe light. Lowell was right. She had to get out of here. Fast.

He stepped aside and opened his arm to her, letting her scurry out first. Teagan ducked her head and her hair fell over her face, shielding her. The moment she was cloaked in the deserted safety of the hallway, she stuffed her thumbnail into her mouth and started to gnaw. If she didn't gnaw, she was going to cry. And crying was not an option. So much for the manicure.

"Teagan!" her father called out.

"Michael, let her go," Karen said in a calming tone. "Leave her alone for a few minutes."

You better listen to her, Teagan thought, turning the corner and shoving open the door to the bridal suite. *You come back here and I cannot be responsible for my actions.*

Teagan was in a rage. A blind, irrational rage. The

moment the door closed behind her and George Lowell, she whirled on him like a tornado.

"I want that waitress fired this second!" she shouted. "Her and that idiot boy-band-looking valet that walked me in here. I don't know where the hell you hire your people from, but I have never seen service like this outside of Red Lobster."

"Miss Phillips, please calm down," Lowell said, raising his hands like stop signs. He didn't back up or get flustered, which just irritated Teagan more.

"I'll calm down when you fire their asses!" she snapped. "Do you have any idea how much this dress cost? More than you make in a month!"

Lowell had the decency to go pale. "Accidents happen, Miss Teagan. I—"

"Why are you still here?" Teagan practically screamed. "That's it! I'm gonna sue this place for all it's worth! You can't just destroy someone's personal property and then stand there and tell me about accidents!" she added, barely even aware of what she was saying. "I'll call my lawyer right now!"

Teagan didn't have her own lawyer, of course, but Lowell didn't know that. She found her bag sitting on the vanity table and rifled through it for her phone. In her blind fury, however, she couldn't find it and her frustration only mounted.

"Miss Phillips, please. I'll go talk to the waitress," George Lowell said finally. "I'll . . . I'll do as you request. Just please, try to take a few breaths and calm down."

"Fine," Teagan said, stepping away from her bag. Her hands were trembling.

"I'll be right back to help you get cleaned up," Lowell told her. Then he turned and slipped soundlessly out of the room.

The second he was gone, Teagan burst into tears. She

couldn't help it anymore. Her reflection wavered three times over in the concave mirrors, the huge red stain like a gash of blood down her body. This wasn't happening. It could not be happening.

Teagan grabbed a tissue box off the vanity table and yanked out a huge wad of tissues. She pulled the neckline of her dress away from her body and dug down with the tissues, wiping at her stained skin. Half a cup of cocktail sauce came out with the tissues and she grimaced, tossing the whole mess toward the garbage can and missing by a mile. Her chest was heaving up and down so hard she felt like she was going to vomit. The dress was ruined beyond repair. Her specially commissioned sweet sixteen dress. What had she done to deserve this?

"Okay, that's it," Teagan said aloud when she heard the direction her thoughts were going. She took a deep breath and wiped her fingers under her eyes. She refused to feel sorry for herself. She refused to let anyone know she had cried.

Teagan stared at her reflection in the mirror. What was she supposed to do now? She couldn't go back out there like this. But she couldn't admit defeat and go home either, no matter how much her Juicy sweats and cashmere blankets were calling out to her.

Another deep breath and Teagan had formulated a plan. She searched her gigantic purse patiently this time and found her phone. She only paused for a moment when she saw that it wasn't on. She must have forgotten to reboot it after the salon. As soon as it sprang to life, it beeped happily at her, letting her know she had several messages. Apparently her father *had* tried to call her all day. As if she cared. She hit the speed dial button for the kitchen phone.

"Hello, Miss Teagan! How is the party?" Mrs. Natsui asked.

"It sucks. You need to get down here and bring me some dresses from my closet," Teagan said, pacing back and forth in front of the mirror.

"What? What happened to your lovely blue—"

"Do you have a pen or what?" Teagan snapped impatiently.

There was a split second of silence. "Yes, miss."

"Good. Bring me the pink Moschino, the blue Vivienne Tam, and the flowered Gaultier that's still in the bag. Got it?" Teagan asked.

"Yes, Miss Teagan," Mrs. Natsui replied.

Teagan looked at her shoes and sighed. "I'm also going to need my silver Mizrahi sling backs and the hot pink stilettos I got in New York last month."

"All right, Miss Teagan."

"Get Jonathan to drive you over here ASAP," Teagan said. "And wrap everything in plastic! It's raining."

"I know, Miss Teagan," Mrs. Natsui said, an edge in her sickly sweet voice. What was with everyone and the attitude today?

Natsui's statement was punctuated by a flash of lightning and a rumble of thunder. Teagan hung up on her. She knew from experience that the more she talked back to Natsui, the slower the woman moved.

Teagan dropped her phone in her large bag and slipped the straps over her shoulder. She was proud to note that now that she had taken some action, the tears had completely dried up. The clothing situation was taken care of. Now all she had to do was locate some alcohol. She knew it was here somewhere and her bag was just big enough to smuggle a couple of bottles back to the party. Her father was not going to get the last word on this matter. There was no way she was going through the rest of this night without getting plastered. Hello? She was supposed to have sex tonight! Her dear old dad had no idea how much his one phone call to the club had ruined.

Taking a deep breath, Teagan slipped out into the hall and headed away from the ballroom. She dimly recalled from the tour she and her father had taken of the club a few years ago that they had a tremendous wine cellar stocked with all the greats. The vodka and bourbon and scotch were probably all under lock and key somewhere—that was, if this club knew anything about its over-privileged, out-for-mischief teenage clientele. But they probably never thought that Teagan and her friends would go trolling for Shiraz. She was, in fact, counting on it.

At the end of the corridor, the hallway split off in two directions. Every wall sconce trembled with each downbeat blasting from Shay's woofers. A raucous group cheer went up from the ballroom. Apparently everyone was having fun without her. Well, not for long. Teagan looked left and right, then hooked the right, just hoping she had chosen well. She nearly jumped in triumph when she found a door clearly marked *Wine Cellar.*

Ha! Think you can ruin my night? Teagan thought, picturing her smug father. She said a silent prayer as she reached for the doorknob. Mercifully it turned and the door swung open, letting out a cool gust of stale air.

Teagan flipped the light switch, but nothing happened. She tried it a few more times, but still the stubborn fluorescent fixture above the stairs refused to respond. Blowing out a frustrated sigh, Teagan stepped onto the first wooden step and closed the door behind her, plunging herself into total darkness.

There has to be another light downstairs, she told herself, shivering. She clutched her bag to her side and started her descent. The steps let out a loud, lazy whine as she took each one carefully. One board felt like it was bending under her weight. Unbelievable. She wasn't *that* huge. Couldn't this stupid club afford a new set of steps for its precious wine cellar?

There was no railing to speak of, so Teagan put her hands out for balance, squinting into the dark.

I can't believe this is my sweet sixteen, she thought, holding her breath. *My life sucks. I have no mother, my father hates me, and I have been reduced to raiding the wine cellar on the biggest night of my life. Everyone is against me. My dad, Karen, that idiot George Lowell. I bet the waitress meant to slam into me. She was probably jealous and wanted to ruin my night. I hope she cries when he fires her. I hope she begs and pleads and—*

Teagan felt the heel of her shoe catch, but she couldn't stop her other foot from going forward. Her stomach swooped as she grasped at the nothingness all around her and pitched forward, tumbling into the darkness. There was a distinct *crack* and Teagan wasn't sure if it was the stairs, her shoe's heel, or her ankle breaking in two. She didn't have more than a second to ponder it, though, because a moment later, after letting out a bloodcurdling scream that was heard by no one, she had tumbled down the last eight stairs and smacked her perfectly coiffed head against the icy concrete floor.

While Shay laid down his signature groove in the ballroom above, Teagan Phillips lay on the basement floor, motionless.

Rosewood Prep Sentinel

OP - ED PAGE

Issue: The Biggest Story of the Year?
Please.

Teagan Phillips is having a sweet sixteen. Have you heard? Yeah. Thought so. It's all anyone can seem to wrap their tongue around these days. People are talking about it in the computer lab. In the locker room. In the student lounge. In the mall. In the freakin' frozen food section of the supermarket. What are they going to wear? Who are they going to go with? What are they going to give the all-important guest of honor?

I ask you, fellow students, is this what we have come to? Do we really, as intelligent young people who will soon become functioning members of today's society, have nothing more important to converse about? The world does not revolve around Teagan Phillips. Our lives do not revolve around her. This *school* does not revolve around her. I mean, come on! She's not even a nice *person*. She doesn't need all of us talking about her and inflating her ego. What she really needs is a solid smack upside the head. Maybe then she'd wake up and realize that living for her sweet sixteen is just pathetic.

But *you're* all living for *her* party, so what does that make you? Freaky, huh? Think about it.

I suggest you get your butts to the school lobby, read the activities board, and find something worthy of spending your time on. There's an Amnesty International meeting after school on Thursday. The women's lacrosse team is in the county finals this weekend. Rama Gupta and Akiko San are *both* competing in the state piano competition in Harrisburg next week. These people are *real* people with *real* talents. People worth getting excited about. I hope to start hearing some mention of *them* in the hallways, in place of a certain other spoiled someone whom I won't even mention again so that I can start stopping the madness now.

Thank you for your time,

Ariana Metz

Freshman

Retort: The Biggest Story of the *Year*? YES!

Ariana Metz is just bitter because she's a freshman and was not invited to the party.

Teagan Phillips

Sophomore

Chapter 8

"Teagan? Teagan, wake up."

Teagan felt like she was sleeping the sleep of a cold patient who had chugged too much NyQuil. She could hear the voice trying to wake her, but it was like slogging through low-fat peanut butter trying to bring herself out of it.

"Teagan? Are you all right?"

Suddenly she recognized the voice and wrenched open her eyes. The cold, acrid air rushed in on her. She squinted in the darkness, her heart pounding. "Mom?"

A sharp pain stabbed her in the back of the head and she closed her eyes again, the earth spinning beneath her. Shakily she brought her hand to her forehead and at the same time felt her leg twisted beneath her at an odd angle. She straightened her knee, wincing in pain, and took a deep breath. Again the pain in her skull assaulted her.

"Can you sit up?" a voice in the darkness asked.

Teagan narrowed her eyes and a face came into focus,

hovering above her. Not her mom. Not at all. This woman had thick dark hair with chunky blond highlights that were just begging for a touch-up. Purple splotches surrounded her green eyes and she had a white bandage taped to her chin. At least her black suit was of high quality. Probably an Ellen Tracy.

Struggling up to her elbows, Teagan tried to ignore the throbbing in her skull. Lying off to the side was her one unstained Jimmy Choo, the heel snapped in half. Teagan rolled her eyes and winced again.

Just kill me now, she thought.

"Are you all right?" the woman asked again. She turned around and yanked the cord on a swinging bare bulb. Teagan blinked against the sudden influx of light.

"No, I'm not all right," Teagan snapped back, pushing herself onto her bare knees. Damn, the floor was freezing cold. The woman offered her a hand, but Teagan ignored it and pressed her fingers into the concrete, shoving herself off the ground. She teetered for a moment on her one shoe and when she pressed her other foot into the ground, she realized she had sprained her ankle.

"Oh. Mother—"

"I don't think you want to finish that sentence," the woman said.

"Oh, you don't think so, do you?" Teagan asked. She braced one hand against the wall and removed her other shoe, tossing the once-precious couture item across the room. "Well, let me tell you what *I* think. I think I'm going to sue this place for all it's worth. Do you have any idea what you and your idiot staff have put me through tonight? And no light or handrail on the stairs? You people are just *begging* for it!"

The whole time Teagan was shouting, her head screamed with pain and her ankle pulsated like it had its own heart. The injuries only fueled the fire. Unfortunately, the woman didn't appear the least bit intimidated. She was, in fact, regarding Teagan with interest, her head tilted to one side. Like she was studying the windows at Barneys, deciding whether or not to go in. Teagan found it to be seriously unnerving.

"Do you have any idea why you're so angry?" the woman asked her with the clinical tone of a general practitioner.

"What are you, insane?" Teagan shouted. "Of course I do! My father defecated all over my sweet sixteen, my Vera Wang is trashed, I just fell down the stairs, and now my Jimmy Choos are Dumpster bound too. Doesn't take a genius to figure it out."

The woman shook her head, a slight smile playing about her lips, and pulled her hair back from her shoulders. As she did so, Teagan noticed the glint of a slim silver chain around the woman's neck. A small white crystal dangled just above the top button of the woman's suit jacket. Teagan leaned forward to inspect it and was hit with a wave of nausea and dizziness so sudden and fierce she fell back against the cool cinder block wall.

Please don't let me barf on my dress too, Teagan thought, breathing deeply in and out until the dizziness subsided. She braced her hands over her knees and her stomach grumbled audibly. The woman laughed.

Teagan suddenly went hot all over. In an instant she remembered why she was down here in the first place. Wine. She needed some wine to dull the pain in her skull and ankle and to shut up her stupid stomach. A nice hearty red. Something expensive.

She looked around, ready to grab the first bottle she saw, but realized there were no bottles to speak of. No shelves with little dips cut out of them. No nothing. This wasn't a wine cellar at all but a dusty, box-filled storage cellar.

The sign on the door had said *Wine Cellar*. Where the hell was all the wine?

"What you're looking for isn't here," the woman said, her voice almost kind.

"Yeah, and how the hell do you know what I'm looking for?" Teagan snapped.

"Trust me. I know," the woman said, taking a step toward her. Once the woman was standing fully in the light, Teagan could see that she might have once been pretty. Still could have been if she wasn't so haggard around the edges and if she got a decent stylist who would have talked her out of those awful streaks. "Come on," the woman said. "I'll take you where you want to go."

Finally, Teagan thought. The woman reached for Teagan's arm, but Teagan snatched it away. She was not about strangers touching her.

The woman shrugged and led the way up the stairs. "Just watch. There's a knot in the eighth step," she said over her shoulder.

"Now you tell me," Teagan said under her breath. She grabbed her purse off the floor and trudged barefoot after her, luckily at least her ankle was feeling a little better.

The woman held the door for Teagan, who reveled in the warmth as she stepped out onto the floral carpet. She glanced at the door as it closed, ready to lace into the woman about the incorrect signage, but held her tongue at the last second. The sign on the door clearly read *Storage Cellar*. Teagan blinked, confused. She really hadn't thought she was *that* buzzed.

"This way," the woman said, starting down the hall.

Teagan looked down at her dress as she followed the woman. The cocktail sauce had dried, forming a thick crust on the skimpy material. One of her toes was still stained red. She couldn't wait to get a little warming wine in her and clean herself up. She pulled out her cell phone and checked the time, wondering how long it would be until Natsui got her butt over here. Over half an hour had passed since she had phoned her maid.

God. Was I really knocked out? Teagan wondered.

The woman grabbed a golf umbrella out of a closet near the end of the hall and started for an exit door.

"We're going *outside?*" Teagan asked, shoving her phone back into her bag.

"That's where we need to go," the woman said.

Teagan rolled her eyes. Did this woman enjoy being cryptic? "Fine, but let's make it quick. I kind of have a party to go to."

"I know," the woman said.

She opened the door and raised the umbrella. Teagan ducked under it and stepped out into the thunderstorm. They were standing at the edge of the parking lot. Hundreds of luxury cars were lined up in rows along with dozens of limos with their cab seat lights on, the drivers chilling out inside, smoking cigarettes and listening to ESPN radio.

"Okay, I'm having a moment," Teagan said. "Where are you taking me?"

Suddenly another door slammed and out walked Teagan's inept waitress, cursing under her breath.

"Spoiled brat bitch," the woman muttered.

"Ugh!" Teagan gasped indignantly. "Where does she get off?"

The former waitress struggled with a cheap umbrella, shoving the mechanism up and down to no avail. The canopy refused to open.

"Unbelievable!" the woman shouted at the sky. She tossed the whole thing into an overflowing Dumpster, yanked the collar of her jacket over her already-soaked head, and ran for it, weaving around BMWs, Lexus SUVs, and Jaguars on her way to the employee lot at the other end.

"Yeah! That's right! Get in your Subaru and go back to your tenement!" Teagan shouted into the rain. Who did that woman think she was, calling Teagan a bitch? *She* was the one who had ruined Teagan's dress and her entire night. It wasn't Teagan's fault that the waitress was totally inept. Some people were just so clueless.

"Nice. Very ladylike," the woman said to her.

"Bite me," Teagan responded. "Where's the wine?"

"This way," the woman said.

Teagan followed her across the corner of the parking lot and onto another flagstone pathway that led toward the gardens behind the club. Her bare feet were freezing and wet and the wind blew the rain sideways, soaking her heels and calves as well. This place better have some damn fine wine in stock or Teagan was going to pull a Lizzie Grubman.

Finally the woman paused in the middle of the pathway and Teagan looked up. "Why are we stopping? I swear this place is going right downhill. Is Lowell just hiring right out of prisons and institutions these days?"

"Funny," the woman said flatly.

"*Where* the *hell* is the *wine cellar?*" Teagan shouted, enunciating her words like she was talking to one of the three scholarship ESL students at Rosewood.

The woman pointed into the rain and Teagan noticed for the first time that they were standing just yards from the gazebo. This was where couples came every spring and summer Saturday to pledge their eternal devotion to each other. She had seen hundreds of romantic photos taken in this very spot when she had browsed through local photographers' portfolios. That was why it took her a second to realize that there was a couple standing in the center of the gazebo right now. It would have looked odd if there *hadn't* been a pair of lovers there.

"Ew," Teagan said when she saw that the two people were locked in a tight embrace. "What are you, a voyeur?"

The couple parted and Teagan felt her knees go weak. Lindsee wiped the back of her hand across her skinny lips and then pressed her ample breasts against Max's waiting chest. She smiled up at him, running her finger down his cheek.

"Oh . . . my . . . God," Teagan said under her breath.

Max, *her* Max, wrapped his arms around Lindsee's waist and kissed her forehead. She nuzzled into him and he rested his chin on top of her golden blond head.

"I missed you, Sweet Bottom," he said, clear as day. Then he reached down and squeezed Lindsee's butt cheeks in both hands. Lindsee giggled and smacked his shoulder, loving every minute of it.

"*She's* Sweet Bottom?!" Teagan screeched, whirling irrationally on the country club worker. "Her butt is *so* much bigger than mine!"

When she turned around again, Max's tongue was halfway

down Lindsee's throat. She couldn't believe they had the audacity to just keep making out like she wasn't even there. This was completely out of control.

"Hey! Slut!" Teagan shouted, rushing toward the gazebo through the rain. She was doused right through her dress in four seconds flat, but she hardly cared. The two cheating, lying, scum-sucking backstabbers didn't even pause for air. "You thought you were leaving *her* a message last night, you total lush?" she shouted. "God! I can't believe I was going to have *sex* with you! We are *so* over!"

Max simply slid his hands up Lindsee's back and pulled her closer to him. Lindsee lifted her leg slightly, rubbing her knee up and down the side of Max's thigh like a dog in heat. Teagan was sure she was going to boot.

"Hello?" she shouted, angry tears filling her eyes. "It's me! Your *girlfriend*?"

"They can't hear you," the woman said, stepping onto the gazebo's bottom stair.

Teagan took no note of her. Max and Lindsee broke apart again and Lindsee fiddled with Max's lapel.

"So, when she tells you she wants to have sex with you, what are you going to say?" she asked coyly.

"Thanks, but no thanks. Not tonight," Max said with a twisted grin. "There's no way she can compare to you."

Teagan felt like she had been shot. She staggered back a few steps and whacked into one of the supporting beams. This couldn't be happening. They couldn't be saying all of this right in front of her like she wasn't even here. Her best friend and her boyfriend. All the things she had shared with them. All the secrets and giggles and intimacies. They couldn't be this cruel.

"But don't break up with her tonight," Lindsee said. She

pulled her compact out of her bag and quickly checked her makeup. "She'll just throw one of her patented fits." She smirked as she snapped the compact closed.

"I know. I'll wait until tomorrow," he said, pulling Lindsee back toward him by the wrist. "I just can't wait until we don't have to sneak around anymore."

"I kind of like the sneaking," Lindsee said slyly.

"All right, that's it!" Teagan shouted. "You want to see a fit!?"

She was just charging toward them when the woman put a surprisingly strong hand down on her shoulder, stopping her cold. Teagan felt like she was going to explode out of her skin.

"Let go of me!" she shouted.

"They can't hear you," the woman said in her ear, sending an odd tingle over her skin. "They can't hear you or see you."

"Omigod, you are so in need of a straitjacket," Teagan said.

"Teagan, trust me. If you stop for one moment and really look inside yourself, you'll know what I'm saying is true," the woman told her. "You're not even in your own body."

Suddenly Teagan felt a shot of cold so intense she could have been dropped through the January ice at Wilson's Pond. Her fingers and toes curled and all the hair on her arms stood at attention. Even her teeth felt cold.

"You're insane," she said, ignoring every instinct in her body.

She lunged forward to grab Lindsee and rip her skinny, betraying lips off Max. But instead of touching Lindsee's dewy flesh, Teagan watched, wide-eyed, as her hand went right *through* Lindsee's skin, into her shoulder, and out her back. It was like shoving her hand into a vat of warm Jell-O, and the sensation finally sent Teagan's already-ravaged stomach over the edge. Gasping for air, Teagan stumbled for the railing and gripped it with all her might, dry heaving into the rosebushes on the other side.

Oh God! I'm dead! Teagan thought wildly, even as her eyes bulged and her throat burned with pain. *I'm dead on my sweet sixteen.*

This was the perfect end to a totally janked-up day.

A warm hand touched her back gently and Teagan managed to stand up. She looked into the tired yet kind eyes of the country club worker.

"Am I a ghost?" she whimpered, trying to prepare herself for the worst. After what she had just felt, she would pretty much believe anything.

"Yes," the woman said in a soothing voice. "I'm sorry to tell you this, Teagan, but you are."

Teagan's knees went out from under her and her butt slammed down on a slim bench that ran along the gazebo's perimeter. Her mind swam. She tried to breathe but couldn't. Instantly her heart started to spasm and she put her hand to her chest, gasping with all her might.

I'm dead, she thought. *I'm really dead.*

"It's okay, Teagan," the woman said, coming over and laying her warm hands on Teagan's bare shoulders. She bent over until they were eye to eye. "Look into my eyes and breathe. It's going to be okay."

"Are you insane?!" Teagan screeched. "I'm dead! Nothing's ever going to be okay!"

Her gut twisted in pain and she doubled over, pressing her forehead into the cold, wet surface of the gazebo's railing. She clung to it with both hands, desperate to touch anything real. Anything that could make her believe that she was still here—still alive. That this was all just some kind of screwed-up nightmare.

"Wait a minute," she said suddenly, straightening. "If I'm dead, why can you touch me? Why can I touch this?" she asked, slapping her hand against one of the support beams.

"We can touch each other because I'm a ghost too," the woman said patiently. "Why we can touch inanimate objects, I don't know. I don't make up the rules; I just work here."

"You're a ghost too?" This was all too much to handle. Teagan's eyes welled with hot tears and her nose clogged instantly. "No," she said. "No. I don't believe you. I'm not dead. I can't be dead. I'm only sixteen."

She stalked over to Lindsee and Max, not even caring anymore that they were going at it right in front of her, and screamed at the top of her lungs. "Hey! I'm right here! Come on, you guys! Please!" she shouted, the tears bursting forth. "Please! I don't want to be dead! Just hear me!"

"They can't," the ghost told her, touching her shoulders again from behind. "The sooner you accept this, Teagan, the easier this night will be."

"Easier? What the hell are you talking about?" Teagan shouted, whirling on her fellow ghost as tears streamed down her face. "You're standing here, telling me that I'm *dead*."

"I know. It took a while for me to accept it too," the woman told her. "But we have to. We have to move on. And soon."

"Move . . . move on?" Teagan asked timidly, her stomach turning. "Like, to where? To heaven?"

"Not exactly."

Teagan dry-heaved. "To hell? Come on! I haven't been *that* bad!"

"Oh yeah, you have," the woman said with a smirk. "But we're not going there either. I have some things to show you."

Teagan swallowed against the hollow fear in her chest. "What?" she asked, imagining every freaky Halloween movie she had ever seen. Images of graveyards and fiery dimensions and skeletal demons in black robes filled her mind.

"You'll see," the woman told her.

"Oh no, Cryptic Chick," Teagan said, wiping her cheeks quickly and taking a deep breath. She slid along the railing, backing in a circle around the two people who had betrayed her. She had to stall. She had to think this through. "I . . . I want to deal with these two first. They can't get away with this! Don't I get a dying wish?" she blurted.

I can't believe this. I can't believe I just said that. I'm dead. I'm no longer of the living. This can't actually be—

"Teagan—"

"I mean, *Lindsee*?" she shouted, clinging to a subject she could actually wrap her brain around. "She's totally pushing stuffed-sausage status in that dress! How the hell is *she* Sweet Bottom?"

It wasn't true, of course. Lindsee was looking as gorgeous and elegant as ever. But Teagan could think of nothing else to do at the moment but tear the girl down.

"Can't I just stick around here and haunt them or something?" she asked weakly.

"Teagan, you shouldn't have wasted so much time on these superficial relationships," the woman answered with a sorrowful shake of her head. "On these people who didn't really care for you. Especially when there were people out there who did." She reached for Teagan's hand. "We need to go."

Teagan didn't like this. She didn't like all this use of the past tense. She held both hands against the congealed stain on her dress and trembled so hard she felt like her body was going to fall apart. "Where?" she asked again.

"You'll see," the woman said.

Teagan glanced at the two people making out next to her. They were still alive. Warm and happy and alive. She was dead in a basement and they were making out like their lives depended on it. It wasn't fair. Nothing was fair.

"I'm scared," Teagan said without thinking.

"I know. But I'll be with you," the woman said, finally taking Teagan's hand in hers. "Trust me. It's going to be okay. Eventually."

Instantly Teagan felt a warm whoosh of air blow her skirt up Marilyn Monroe style and just like that, she faded to nothing.

Rosewood Prep Sentinel

GOSSIP PAGE

Weekly Poll

By Laura Wood, Senior Writer

In case you haven't heard (yeah, right), Teagan Phillips's sweet sixteen will be held a week from this Saturday at the Upper Sheridan Country Club. Now, we all know that the bigger the party, the better the chance it will degenerate into total mayhem. So for this week's poll, we thought we'd ask the obvious. How, exactly, do you think this night of nights will end? Here's how you, our faithful readers, answered:

In an orgy:	76%
In a DEA raid:	10%
With several select members of the senior class being hauled off to jail:	9%
With the country club burned to the ground:	3%
Peacefully:	0%
Other:	2%

Our favorite other vote: With Teagan Phillips lying facedown in a pool of her own vomit.

Chapter 9

"Okay, what the hell was that?" Teagan asked, yanking herself away from the ghost. Her skin sizzled. Every millimeter of her body was buzzing and she felt like her very cells were bouncing around inside her, reorganizing themselves. Teagan had never felt anything so disturbing. If her cells were reorganizing, didn't that mean that they had temporarily been *dis*organized?

"Just a very efficient way to travel," the ghost said with a shrug.

"Travel where?" Teagan asked, happy to note that there was no fire and brimstone. She adjusted the strap of her bag on her shoulder and looked around the very familiar if small entryway. "Wait a minute, I know this house," she said with a rush of nostalgia. "This is Emily's house, right?"

Laughter erupted from the living room off to Teagan's left and her pulse accelerated. "What the hell are we doing here?" she asked.

"Go check it out," the ghost said, lifting her bandaged chin.

Teagan turned and stepped tentatively over the threshold and into the small dining room. She had spent so much time in this house when she was little that she knew every nook and cranny, even though she hadn't been there in a couple of years. This place had been like her second home, but now that she was back, she felt like a complete outsider. Life had clearly gone on here without her.

The table in the dining room was set with paper plates. Streamers hung from the ceiling. There were colorful balloons everywhere. It looked just like a kindergartner's birthday party was taking place, but there were no five-year-olds in sight. Gathered on the couch and chairs in the living room just behind the dining area were Emily and a bunch of her friends. Emily looked a lot like she had the last time Teagan had seen her, at the end of eighth grade—just a touch older. Her blond hair fell in waves over the shoulders of her light pink T-shirt. Her face was makeup free, but her cheeks were flushed and her blue eyes bright. She had always been one of the most naturally pretty people Teagan had known.

Strung behind the couch over Emily's head was a glittering pink sign that read *Happy Birthday, Sweet Sixteen!*

Teagan's jaw dropped. "*This* is Emily's sweet sixteen?" she asked, scrunching up her nose. "I feel so bad for her."

"Yeah. You go with that," the ghost said sarcastically.

"This is weird," Teagan said, passing in front of a pair of girls who were chowing down on chips and salsa. They didn't so much as blink as she brushed by two inches away. It was kind of cool, actually, being able to move among people like this unseen. Teagan would have much preferred not to be dead, of course, but if she had to be dead, this was definitely turning out to be a perk.

"I know, right?" the ghost said. "Let's stand over here."

They took a spot near the wall. Teagan hugged herself, wondering what the hell they were doing at Emily's birthday party. Was this what people did when they died? Dropped in on old friends? That was all well and good, but if she was going to be at someone's sweet sixteen, she would much rather be at her own. She might be dead—still getting used to that—in the basement, but she had worked long and hard on her party. The least this ghost could give her was the chance to see how it all turned out.

Plus this new invisibility thing could work in her favor. She could spy on people and find out what they really thought. By now they *had* to be talking about how much cooler her bash was than Shari Marx's.

"You want to go back to the country club, don't you?" the ghost asked.

Teagan balked. "How did you know that?"

"Why don't you just try to focus, okay? You're here for a reason," the ghost said impatiently.

"You're not gonna bother telling me what that reason is, though, right?" Teagan asked sarcastically

The ghost rolled her eyes. "Let's get this straight right now. Your little party? It doesn't matter anymore."

"Hey, I may be dead, but I still worked my butt off on that thing! Why can't we just—"

"Shut it!" the ghost said, motioning to zip her lip. Teagan's mouth snapped shut and she slumped against the wall, petulant.

I just died, for freak's sake, she thought. *How about a little sympathy?*

"Here! Open this one! Me and Meredith chipped in for it!"

An African-American girl with a long ponytail handed Emily a wrapped gift. Emily's friends watched eagerly as Emily tore into the package. Piled up on the floor at her feet were the presents she had already opened. A white sweater. A couple of books. Some jewelry boxes from Macy's and Claire's. A Phillies baseball cap. Nothing Teagan would ever touch, let alone wear.

A little boy in blue jeans and a SpongeBob T-shirt ran around the room, waving some kind of dragon toy in the air and weaving around people's legs. A totally gorgeous older guy with wide shoulders and pecs that were visible even through his cotton sweater reached down and caught the kid around the waist, tickling him until he screamed.

"Damn! Is that Gary?" Teagan asked, shocked. "Somebody's been working out!"

The last time she had laid eyes on Emily's older brother—the boy who had followed her around like a puppy dog her entire young life—his skin had been starting to break out and he was on his way from scrawny to pudgy. This Gary was a major improvement. Yum-*mee*.

"Gary, could you take Ricky upstairs and show him your new video games?" Emily's mother asked from her spot in the doorway.

"Sure, Mom," Gary said, placing the kid back on the floor. "Come on, Ricky. Wanna play some Madden?"

"Yeah!"

"Who the heck is Ricky? Did Emily's parents have another kid?" Teagan asked.

"No. He's a cousin," the ghost replied.

"How do you know?" Teagan asked.

The ghost shrugged. "I know lots of things."

Emily ripped open the paper on her gift and revealed a black box from The Limited. "Oh my gosh! You guys didn't!"

"They chipped in for something from The Limited?" Teagan asked, confused. "What kind of budget do their parents put them on?"

The girl who had handed her the gift shared a grin with Meredith Griffin across the way. Teagan remembered Meredith from grade school. She was pretty and had totally grown into her once too-tall frame.

Emily lifted out a flowered sundress and squealed with delight. "You guys! Thank you *so* much!" she said, getting up to hug Meredith and her friend. "It's too much! You didn't have to do that!"

"It's your sweet sixteen!" Meredith exclaimed.

"Yeah! It was worth the extra shift," the other girl said.

"Well, thank you," Emily said. "I've been coveting this dress for a month."

"Hold it up!" her father called out, wielding his camera.

Emily held the dress against her body and struck a pose. Everyone clapped and Emily blushed. When she sat back down again, the cute boy sitting next to her wrapped his arm around her shoulders.

"You should wear that on our date tomorrow night," he said.

"Totally," Emily replied, giving him a quick kiss on the cheek.

"Whooo!" a few of the girls catcalled, laughing.

"None of that now! There are parents present!" Emily's mom joked.

Emily smiled and got back to the gift opening.

"Huh. Emily's got a boyfriend," Teagan said, checking him out. He was wearing a rugby shirt and baggy jeans and sporting a way too short crew cut. But he had warm brown eyes and a nice smile. Plus he couldn't seem to take his eyes off his girlfriend, unlike some boys Teagan knew. "Not too shabby."

"Hey, Em! Whatever happened to that girl you used to share your parties with?" a red-haired girl asked. She looked vaguely familiar, but Teagan didn't know her name. Must have been one of Emily's friends from soccer whom she always used to invite to their parties.

"What was her name again? Tanya . . . ?"

"Ew! Tanya!?" Teagan said with a grimace.

"Teagan," Emily said, lifting a gift bag onto her lap. "Actually, she's having some huge party over at the country club tonight."

"Ooh-ooh," a couple of the girls said facetiously. Teagan saw Jennifer Robbins, a former classmate and friend, actually push her own nose into the air, earning laughs from the guys around her.

"She was such a snob," Meredith said. "I'm glad she ended up at Rosewood."

"Hey!" Teagan said, standing up straight.

"She's not that bad," Emily said.

"Please! She almost ran over my mom's dog with her little convertible last week and she didn't even stop," Elena Christiansen said. "My mom almost had a heart attack."

"That was *her* mom? They were definitely *not* in the cross-walk," Teagan said. "And I checked the rearview mirror to make sure they were okay!"

"She was probably late for her lip wax," someone joked, earning serious laughter.

Teagan blushed furiously. "It was a bikini wax," she said under her breath.

"Come on, you guys. Be nice," Emily said. "I think she's just really lonely. Her mom died when we were little and I don't think she has a lot of real friends."

"Cry me a river," Jennifer said, rolling her eyes.

"Bite me," Teagan grumbled.

"I don't know. I feel bad for her," Emily said, though she was smiling at the jokes.

"*You* feel bad for *me*!?" Teagan blurted, shaking. "I have a world-renowned chef cooking dinner for me right now! I have fifty waiters catering to my guests! I have three hundred people at *my* party! What do *you* have?"

"Um, Teagan? She can't hear you," the ghost said.

"Well, where does she get off?" Teagan cried, whirling on the ghost.

"Actually, you may have more people at your party, but so far, not one of them has come to look for you and you've been down in that basement for . . . almost an hour," she said, consulting her gold watch.

Teagan's heart sank. "Oh, that's nice," she said. "Kick the dead girl while she's down."

"Just stating the truth," the ghost told her.

"Well, how do you know that no one's come looking for me?"

"Like I said, I just know things."

"You're kind of obnoxious, you know that?" Teagan said sarcastically.

"I forget, are you the pot or the kettle right now?" the ghost shot back.

Teagan narrowed her eyes. Hell was starting to look like a viable option.

"I don't get what we're doing here," Teagan snapped.

"You will," the ghost replied.

"You know . . . we may actually get all the swank details about Teagan's party later," Emily told her friends with a mischievous smile. "My aunt is working it right now."

As she said these last words, a woman stepped into the room and everyone looked up. "Not anymore!" the new arrival announced.

Teagan's heart hit the floor and her hand went to the dried stain on her dress. Standing in the doorway to Emily's living room was the evil waitress. The waitress George Lowell had fired on her behalf.

"Aunt Catherine? What are you doing here?" Emily asked.

"Your little friend got me fired," Aunt Catherine said, ripping off her soaked jacket.

Oh. My. God.

No wonder she had looked so familiar to Teagan. She could see it now, bright as day. The resemblance between Emily's mother and aunt was unmistakable. The aunt was a little rougher around the edges and was twenty pounds heavier—plus she was sporting a bad dye job—but other than that, they could have been twins.

"I got Emily's aunt fired," Teagan said quietly, disbelievingly.

"What?" Mrs. Zeller said.

"Yeah! *She* slammed into *me* and dumped my tray and *I* get fired!" Catherine cried.

"No way!" Teagan shouted. "That was *not* my fault."

"Actually, it kind of was," the ghost replied matter-of-factly.

"And I was supposed to talk to my boss about that promotion tonight," Catherine ranted, shoving her hand through her bangs. "I was going to see about getting an apartment and getting me and Ricky out of your hair, but now . . ."

Emily's mother reached out to rub her sister's arm. "Don't

worry, Cat," she said. "We'll figure something out. And you know we love having you and Ricky here. You don't have to worry about that."

"Well, at least I got outta there with these," Catherine said, pulling a pair of Gucci sunglasses out of her purse. "We could probably sell 'em on eBay."

Teagan felt a twinge of indignation but squelched it. She couldn't believe that the klutzy waitress was Emily's aunt. What were the chances?

Catherine took a deep breath and looked around. She seemed to realize for the first time that there were other people in the room. Emily was ashen and all of her friends had fallen into an uncomfortable silence.

"Oh, jeez. I'm sorry, Em," Catherine said, sniffling noisily. "I interrupted your party."

"It's okay," Emily said, trying for bright but sounding meek.

"No, you go ahead with your presents," Catherine said, waving her hands. "I'll be upstairs."

She turned and rushed out of the party, her steps heavy on the carpeted stairs.

"Still feel sorry for your old friend?" Meredith said.

Unbelievable, Teagan thought. Was *this* why the ghost had brought her here? So she could listen to these people bad-mouth her? How was *she* supposed to know that the klutzy waitress was related to her former best friend? That she had a little kid at home?

"I'd better go talk to Cat," Emily's mother said.

"No. Let me go," Emily told her, standing. She handed her unopened gift to her boyfriend. "I'll be right back."

Emily looked numb and dumbfounded as she picked her way over balls of crumpled wrapping paper and plastic plates of pizza crust. All Emily's friends watched her go. Teagan was the only one of them able to follow.

On the way to Emily's room at the back of the second floor, Emily paused at the door to Gary's bedroom. Inside, Ricky sat on Gary's lap on the end of the twin bed, gripping a PlayStation controller. He continually ran his running back into the guys on the sidelines and laughed every time. There was a cot set up next to the bed with ill-fitting sheets. A teddy bear sat in the center. Clearly Ricky had been bunking with Gary.

Emily sighed and moved on to her room. Catherine was sitting on the bottom bunk, her head in her hands. An open suitcase sat against the wall, all the clothes inside twisted and clumped. Teagan stood back while Emily entered quietly. The room was small enough when only one person was living in it. Now there was no space for anything. Emily sat on a pile of laundry at her aunt's feet.

"Hey," Catherine said, sniffling and trying to stop her tears.

Emily stretched up and pulled a tissue box off the edge of her desk. She handed it to her aunt.

"You'll find another job," she said.

"It's not that easy," her aunt replied, bringing a tissue to her red nose. "And I was already moving up at this one. To start all over someplace else . . ."

"Don't worry about it," Emily said. "You'll be fine."

"Yeah, and in the meantime the creditor bastards are gonna start calling again and Ricky and I are gonna have to keep imposing on you guys," Catherine said, her eyes drooping.

"It's okay," Emily said, reaching out and touching her aunt's leg. "We love having you guys here."

"Yeah, right," the woman said with a scoff.

"We do!" Emily said.

Teagan could practically feel the desperation coming off Emily. Like she *had* to say the right thing and convince this woman to keep freeloading. She was acting like the parent, not the teenage niece. What was going on here?

"Aunt Catherine, it's not your fault Uncle Johnny died," Emily said, her eyes imploring. "It's not your fault you have all those bills."

"I should have had a real job when it happened," Catherine answered, shaking her head and staring down at the tissue. "I should have had insurance."

"But you didn't and now you're stuck and we're helping you," Emily said. "That's what we're here for. There's no point in looking back." Catherine sucked in a shaky breath and a few more tears squeezed out. "Come on! What happened to Miss Positive? Miss Turning Over a New Leaf?"

Catherine grabbed the black faux leather purse from the floor. "She got fired," she said. She opened the huge sack and started rifling through it violently. Finally she found what she was looking for. A lighter and a pack of cigarettes.

Emily sat back, her expression slack. "I thought you quit."

"Yeah, well, I quit a lot of things and it hasn't gotten me anywhere," Catherine said, lighting up.

She stood up and stepped over Emily to get to the window, which she jammed open. She exhaled a stream of blue smoke into the rainy night. Emily turned green.

"Go back to your party, kid," Catherine said gruffly.

Emily stood up and grabbed the door. Teagan stepped out of the way. She saw Emily take one last look at her aunt, then turn her gaze to the floor and walk out.

"What does she mean, she's quit a lot of things?" Teagan asked the ghost once Emily was gone. "Is she a lush or something? Oh! Was she drinking tonight? Is that what made her go all Teri Hatcher on me?"

"No, she's not an alcoholic," the ghost said, gazing at the solitary figure by the window. "She used to be a drug addict, but she kicked it when Ricky was just a baby. She wanted to make a better life for her kid, but with her record it was hard for her to get a job. So when her husband died, she came here to start over."

"She owes a lot of money?" Teagan asked.

The ghost nodded. "Hospitals, credit cards, funeral home," she said. "Between all that, the mourning, and getting fired, I'd say she's officially in danger of backsliding."

"Oh, and I guess that's *my* fault," Teagan said. "I didn't make her a klutz."

"But you did insist she get fired for ruining your precious Vera Wang," the ghost said. "Which, by the way, you never would have worn again even though you spent enough money on it to feed a small village."

Teagan swallowed. She watched Catherine take another drag. Then the woman leaned her elbow on the windowsill and stared out into space.

"Can you tell what she's thinking?" she asked, her heart feeling a bit heavy.

"I'm not a mind reader," the ghost said.

"You knew what *I* was thinking before," Teagan pointed out.

"Well, maybe you're just that transparent," the ghost replied.

She reached out and took Teagan's hand in hers.

* * *

"Stop doing that!" Teagan cried, dizziness overwhelming her as her bare feet touched solid ground once again.

"Sorry. That's all I got in the way of transportation," the woman told her.

Teagan felt a shiver and looked around. She was standing under the awning in front of the Upper Sheridan Country Club. Rain drenched the flagstone walk and the windowpanes trembled with the beats pounding through Shay's speakers. The ghost took a deep breath of the humid air and tipped her head back. Her chin bandage pulled at her skin in a highly unattractive way.

"What are we doing here?" she asked.

"Well, you said you wanted to come back."

"And *you* said it didn't matter," Teagan replied. She crossed her arms over her chest and glared at her ghoulish tour guide. "What the hell is the point of all this? Why did you take me over to Emily's? Just trying to make me feel guilty for something I can do *nothing* about? At least she's still alive. I'm dead! You know, I'm beginning to think you're just plain evil. I mean, who do you—"

Teagan only paused when she noticed two umbrellas approaching the end of the walk from opposite directions. She recognized Maya's scurrying walk and Ashley's truck-driver gait. Those girls both needed a weekend with Tyra Banks to get their poise in order. But at least they had decided to show up.

Maya and Ashley picked across the stones, playing hop-scotch over the rivers that ran between them. When they finally reached the covered steps, they dropped the umbrellas.

Maya shook her hair back. Ashley let out a frustrated groan, sloughing some wetness off her arm. Teagan took one look at them and gasped, covering her mouth with her hand. It took a split second for Maya and Ashley to finally look at each other. When they did, Maya let out a screech that was perfectly drowned by a rumble of thunder.

Ashley and Maya were now wearing the exact same *red* dress. Teagan realized this must have been the one they had originally bought. The one Lindsee had told her about that morning.

"What are you *wearing*?" Maya wailed, her brown eyes huge.

"What are *you* wearing?" Ashley shouted back.

"I can't believe this! I thought you said you returned it!" Maya said.

"Why should I?" Ashley countered, placing one hand on her hip. "It totally looks better with my coloring."

"Oh, please! It completely washes you out!" Maya shouted.

"Omigod, this is *classic*!" Teagan cried, looking at the ghost, who, for the first time, seemed rather amused herself.

"Go home and change," Ashley said, crossing her arms over her chest.

"You go home and change," Maya replied.

"Ugh!" they both groaned shrilly, throwing their hands up in the air.

"You guys! Come on! Who cares what you're wearing!" Teagan shouted after them, laughing as they both stalked back through the rain. "Come back! You're missing the party!"

Both girls turned at the end of the walk and headed back for the valet stand. Teagan glanced at the ghost, still smiling.

"Okay, maybe you're not totally evil," Teagan told her. "That was kind of fun."

"I know. Those two crack me up," the ghost said mirthfully.

Teagan grasped the bronze handle on the door and swung it open, releasing a rush of cool air.

"Where do you think *you're* going?" the ghost asked.

"Inside. I want to see what everyone else is doing."

"Uh-uh! No way. We still have a lot to do," the ghost said, reaching for Teagan's arm. "I just needed a little break after that whole Catherine thing. Total tearjerker."

Teagan's eyes narrowed as she glared at the slim fingers gripping her flesh. She could feel her ire fill her up from her fingertips all the way down to her toes.

"You can't do this to me!" she ranted. "This is my party! You can't just bring me back here and dangle it in front of me like I'm some dumb dog! You can't tell me what to do!"

"Actually, I can," the woman said.

Her grip on Teagan's arm tightened. Teagan let out an inhuman screech, but it did no good. In a dizzying rush of warmth, they were off once again.

Interview with Teagan Phillips re:
Upcoming Sweet Sixteen Party
Transcript 3

Reporter: Rondé Taylor, Staff Writer,
Rosewood Prep Sentinel

RT: This is Rondé Taylor and I'm sitting here with sophomore Teagan Phillips. Teagan has uh . . . agreed to . . . uh, finish up the interview she started with Melissa Bradshaw as long as she was allowed to choose the reporter. So, Teagan, thanks for picking me. This is my first big assignment.

TP: My pleasure, Rondé. And may I say that of all the freshmen on the staff, you are obviously the most qualified. You play football, right?

RT: (*clears throat*) Uh, yeah. I was the only freshman to make varsity this year.

TP: Well, I'm in the presence of celebrity!

RT: No. *I* am. You're, like, a goddess around here, man.

TP: Well, thanks for saying so.

RT: So, if you could get only one thing for your birthday, what would it be?

TP: World peace?

RT: Really?

TP: (*laughter*) Oh, Rondé. You're so cute. No . . . no. Let's see . . . if I could have only one thing for my birthday, I suppose it would be—

RT: To have your mom there?

TP: (*pause*) What?

RT: Well, I know your mom died when you were little and I know that if *my* mom died, I would just want her around, you know? I *love* my mom. She's the coolest. Birthdays would suck without her homemade chocolate cake. Plus she has this special way of singing "Happy Birthday" that is—

TP: Okay, are you supposed to be answering the questions or am I?

RT: Well, I just . . . I—

TP: 'Cuz I don't really need to hear about how you *might* feel *if* your mom died. I really don't need to hear that. I mean, how do you think that makes *me* feel, Rondé?

RT: Oh. God. Sorry, I—

TP: What is wrong with people? Doesn't anyone ever think of anyone other than themselves?

RT: I'm sorry. Really. I didn't think—

TP: Whatever. I have to go. (*sound of chair scraping back*)

RT: Wait! Oh my God. I'm so sorry! Forget I said anything. I'll ask you something else.

TP: You know what, Rondé? You suck as a reporter. (*rustling sounds*)

RT: Come back! (*sound of door slamming*) Oh, crap.

END OF TAPE 3

Chapter 10

"Take me back right now," Teagan demanded the second she felt whole again. Dizziness overwhelmed her as she tried to focus, but she had to close her eyes. She leaned a hand against a cool wall and braced herself. "Take me back. You have no right to do this to me. I—"

She opened her eyes and was surprised to find herself back in her current bedroom. But before relief could set in, she realized something was wrong. The room wasn't as she had left it. WB posters adorned the walls, and the shelves that should have been stocked with the last three years' worth of W and *Vogue* magazines were overflowing with stuffed animals and kiddie books with pink and blue spines.

"Um, what's going on here?" Teagan asked, swallowing hard.

"We have traveled back in time," the ghost said with a grin. "Pretty cool, huh?"

Teagan stepped shakily away from the wall. "Back in time? To when?"

"To another birthday on which you were a total jerk." The ghost settled into the green-and-white-polka-dotted beanbag chair near the window and watched Teagan with interest.

"What, exactly, makes you think you can talk to me that way?" Teagan snapped.

The ghost opened her mouth, but then they both turned their attention to the shouting voices coming from the hall.

"I can't believe you're doing this to me!"

The door was shoved open so hard it hit the wall and knocked Teagan's fifth-grade honors award off its hook. Teagan backed out of the way quickly and felt a swoop of disbelief. Her twelve-year-old self had just stormed into the room, brown curls sticking out in every direction, skinny arms crossed over her chest. This couldn't be happening. This could not be happening.

"What the hell is this?" Teagan blurted, her mouth going dry.

"Cool, huh?" the ghost replied with a grin.

"Teagan, sweetheart, listen to me." Teagan's father walked into the room now, looking distraught. His hair was slightly longer on top than it was today, but otherwise he appeared the same.

"No! I won't listen to you ever again!" little Teagan screamed.

Her face was boiling red and her eyes looked like they were ready to pop out of her skull. Present-day Teagan recoiled in disgust. Did she really look like that when she got mad? It was highly unattractive. But then again, this scene was pre–J.F. Lazartigue shampoo and somewhere smack in the middle of the metal-mouth years. Scrawny and big-headed, twelve-year-old Teagan was suffering right through her awkward stage.

"It's my birthday!" little Teagan shouted, jutting out her chin. Ugh! So cringe-worthy. Teagan was glad she had since learned how not to accentuate her worst feature. "Why do you have to go to stupid New York on my birthday!?"

"Oh my God! I remember this now!" Teagan said, her heart thumping. Yet another birthday when her father had let her down. "He had that huge meeting and he ditched me the morning of my party."

"Teagan, I don't want to. Believe me," her father said, following little Teagan as she stormed into a corner and stubbornly turned her back to him. "But if I don't go to this meeting, we could lose everything. Don't you want to stay in this house? You love your new room."

Little Teagan was fighting back tears. Present-day Teagan could tell by the way she was stoically gasping for air.

"Mom would never do this to me," little Teagan said. "If she were here, she would *hate* you for going away on my birthday!"

Teagan leaned back against the built-in-bookshelves, feeling weak. She actually remembered saying this to her father. She remembered because even at the age of twelve, she knew it was the one thing she could say that would hurt her father the most. Even at the age of twelve, she wanted him to hurt as much as she was hurting. And she had felt a twinge of guilt the second she said it, but not enough to take it back. She had *wanted* to hurt him.

But of course, the arrow hadn't struck home. If she remembered this day correctly, her father hadn't even reacted.

"God, look at him," the ghost said

Teagan glanced at her father, standing behind her younger self. She watched his face contort with pain. Behind his daughter's back, she saw him cover his eyes with his hand.

Oh. My. God. He did *react. I just didn't see. . . .*

Teagan looked across the room at the ghost, who was staring right through her as if she could read her very thoughts.

"Teagan, I wish your mother was here, but she's not," her father said evenly, squelching his feelings. He reached out to touch little Teagan's shoulder.

Little Teagan jerked away. "At least *she* actually *loved* me," she said.

"Yes, she did," her father told her. "And so do I."

Little Teagan inhaled a shaking breath. "No, you don't. You're going away on my birthday. You hate me."

Teagan's father sat down on the edge of her bed and let out a frustrated sigh. "Teagan, look at me."

No one moved.

"Look at me!" her father snapped gruffly. The sound of his angry voice sent a cold arrow through Teagan's heart, but it had the desired effect on little Teagan. Slowly she turned around, her eyes on the floor.

Her father, clearly feeling guilty over having to yell, reached out and took both little Teagan's hands in his. "You are going to have a lovely birthday party with Emily this afternoon," he said. "And tomorrow, when I get home, we'll go shopping in the city and get you anything you want."

Teagan watched her younger self closely. The little girl's head sank even lower.

"That's what he always does," Teagan said aloud, clinging to her anger in an attempt to keep the guilt at bay. "Got a problem, throw money at it. She couldn't care less about shopping. She wants him."

"You mean *you*," the ghost said. "You want him."

"Yeah, I do," Teagan said, feeling numb. Then she heard

what she had said and she pulled herself up straight. "I mean, I did. I don't need him *now*. I'm used to him not being around. Believe me."

"Yeah, right," the ghost said.

Teagan glared at her.

"You know what we should do right now?" Teagan's father asked, ducking his head and looking up at little Teagan hopefully. "We should do our special birthday dance."

"Holy crap, the birthday dance," Teagan said, feeling a rush of warmth and smiling automatically. "I totally forgot about that! We used to do that every year. This stupid little dance to 'You Are the Sunshine of My Life.'"

"Oh, Dad, *please*," little Teagan said, pulling away from him and crossing her arms over her chest again. "I'm not a baby anymore."

The depth of disappointment on her father's face was devastating.

"But we do it every year," her father said, his face falling.

"Not anymore," little Teagan said in an obnoxiously sarcastic voice that sounded very familiar to present-day Teagan. Hideously familiar. Little Teagan screwed her mouth up into a superior smirk.

"Fine," her father said, standing. His voice had taken on an icy tone. He was clearly hurt and little Teagan wasn't giving him anything to work with. "Your presents are downstairs. Marcia will be here to oversee the party."

"Great," little Teagan said. More sarcasm.

Marcia, Teagan thought with a jolt. *Marcia's here?* Marcia Lupe had been her nanny from before her mother died all the way up until she was almost thirteen. Teagan *loved* that woman. She had been the only person Teagan would even talk to just after her mother died. *I wonder what ever happened to her,* Teagan thought now, disturbed to realize that she had no idea where Marcia even lived today.

"I'll see you when I get back," her father said. He leaned over to kiss little Teagan's forehead, but once again, she pulled away. Her father straightened up and sighed, his lips tight. "Happy birthday. I love you."

Then he turned and strode right out the door.

Little Teagan burst into bitter tears—unable to control herself as Teagan was able to years later.

"Poor kid," Teagan said under her breath.

"I know. But he did have to leave," the ghost told her, standing up and joining Teagan as they looked down at her younger self. "Remember? A couple of weeks later at that party your dad threw? You overheard his business partners talking about how he would have lost his company if he hadn't straightened out a problem at the shareholders meeting that weekend."

"How did you know that?" Teagan asked.

"If you stop asking me that, this night's going to be a lot easier," the ghost said with a sigh.

"Okay, fine. Yeah. I did overhear that. But how was I supposed to know that then?" Teagan blurted. "Look at me! I'm just a kid!"

"But old enough to listen," the ghost said. "Old enough to try to understand. Old enough to know how to hurt somebody."

Little Teagan walked over to her bed and pulled her mother's silk birthday scarf out from under her pillow, where it had lived for many years. She balled up the scarf and covered her face with it, sobbing uncontrollably.

Teagan swallowed a lump in her throat. Maybe the ghost

had a point. What kind of person hurt someone intentionally like that? She had known what she was doing, bringing up her mother, and she had done it anyway. Maybe she had been upset. Rightfully upset. But she could have acted like a human. She should have listened to him. She should have let him kiss her good-bye.

"It's different, looking at it from the outside," the ghost said.

"I should have gone after him," Teagan replied. "I should have told him I loved him too. Look at her! Doesn't she realize she wouldn't be so upset if she hadn't acted like such a bitch?"

"Hindsight is twenty-twenty," the ghost said.

Teagan looked at her and rolled her eyes. "Nice cliché."

"It's a cliché for a reason," the woman said, placing her hand on Teagan's shoulder. Then the world faded around Teagan, the sobs of her younger self still choking in her ears.

"Happy *birth*day, dear TeaganandEmily . . . happy birthday to you!"

Teagan and the ghost appeared in the dining room just as the dozens of kids around the table finished up their out-of-tune song. Marcia set the humongous cake down in front of Teagan and Emily, who sat at the very end of the long table.

"Wow. It's really Marcia! It's so weird to see her!" Teagan said, her heart squeezing. Marcia lifted her dark curls over her shoulders and smiled proudly as she stepped back from the cake. Teagan wanted nothing more than to go over and hug the woman—her mother figure for so many years—but she held back. She knew by now that it wouldn't be possible.

"What do you think?" Marcia asked, clasping her hands and looking at the girls.

"It's *beautiful!*" little Emily replied. Little Teagan said nothing.

Emily reached up and adjusted the gold crown that sat jauntily atop her blond curls. Teagan's crown still hung from the back of her chair.

"I can't believe they were still trying to make us wear crowns in sixth grade," Teagan said with a scoff, leaning one arm against the wall. "You can't fault me for refusing to compromise my fashion sense, am I right?"

"Emily's wearing hers," the ghost pointed out.

"Please! So what? That girl would wear anything her mother asked her to wear," Teagan said. "Look at her! Black cords in May? And that pink top is blinding. She's a walking fashion don't."

The ghost blew out a sigh and shook her head.

"What?" Teagan blurted. When she realized she wasn't going to get a rise out of the ghost, she leaned back against the wall to watch the proceedings. It didn't matter what the ghost thought. About this, she knew she was right.

Emily, meanwhile, opened her mouth in awe over the cake. The white butter cream icing was trimmed with pink and yellow flowers. Both their names were written on the top in florid script. Beneath each name were thirteen candles. Twelve for the birthday plus one for luck.

Gary, at this particular time very tall, very skinny, and semi-cute—when he wasn't being a jerk—leaned over from his seat on the side of the table and poked little Teagan on the arm.

"Ow! Stop it!" little Teagan whined.

"Ow! Stop it!" Gary mimicked, making a face.

What a total loser, Teagan thought, recalling all the teasing and bruises she had endured from Gary as the years went on. The whole "when a boy shoves you, it means he likes you" method of flirting.

"Gary! Be good!" Emily's mother said, swiping her hand over his head and mussing his hair.

"I am being good!" he said, poking little Teagan again.

"Ow!"

"Gary!" Emily's father said in his I-mean-business voice.

Emily's mother sighed in frustration. "Okay! Make a wish!" she called out, clearly hoping for some distraction.

Little Teagan stuck out her bottom lip and sat back in her chair, crossing her arms tightly.

"Come on!" Emily said with a laugh. She grabbed for little Teagan's hand. Every year they would hold hands as they made their wishes, thinking it would make the wishes stronger and help them come true. But now little Teagan jerked away from Emily, turning her body sideways so Emily couldn't get ahold of her. Emily's face fell as she gazed uncertainly across the huge expanse of the table at her parents, who hung back by the wall. All the other kids at the table looked at Emily's parents as well.

"Go ahead, baby," Emily's father encouraged her.

Emily shrugged, took a deep breath, and blew out her own candles. Everyone cheered.

"Teagan? Aren't you going to make a wish?" Marcia asked.

"No," little Teagan said stubbornly. "I don't want any cake."

"No. I don't want any cake," Gary mimicked.

Marcia laughed in an embarrassed way and looked at Emily's mom and dad. The two dozen kids gathered at the table stared at the cake, salivating. Finally Marcia leaned down and blew out the candles herself. She picked up the cake and took it back to the kitchen for slicing.

"Ready in five minutes!" she called over her shoulder.

A few impatient groans arose, mostly from the boys who were present. Emily clapped. "I know! Let's play Star Connect!"

"Yeah!" Cassidy Sherman cheered, raising her pudgy hands in fists. "I'll start."

Teagan snorted a laugh. "Cassidy Sherman ruled at Star Connect. She owned like four hundred movies. She even got TiVo before everyone else."

"Josh Hartnett," Cassidy said, looking at the boy sitting next to her.

"Okay, Josh Hartnett was in *Pearl Harbor*," the boy said, looking at Jennifer Robbins.

"Ben Affleck!" Jennifer said, looking proud of herself. "Ben Affleck was in *Pearl Harbor*!"

"Ben Affleck . . . Ben Affleck . . . um . . . *Armageddon!*" Emily said, looking at little Teagan.

Little Teagan just sat there, still in pout mode. Her face was flushed as she pointedly stared at the far wall, away from Emily.

"Come on! You know this!" Teagan said to her younger self, putting her hands out. "*Armageddon!* So easy! Everyone was in that! Liv Tyler! Billy Bob! Owen Wilson! Oh, but did anyone know who Owen Wilson was yet?" she asked the ghost.

"I'm partial to Luke," the ghost said with a one-shouldered shrug.

"Me too!" Teagan cried.

"Teagan? It's your turn," Emily said tentatively.

"So what?"

"She doesn't know!" Gary said, overdoing a laugh. "Oh my God! It's so easy and she doesn't know!" He pointed at Teagan with one hand and the other, over and over again, laughing his butt off.

"I know!" little Teagan said, whacking Gary's hand. "I just don't want to play."

Gary continued to cackle and point, and Teagan could see that her younger self was turning redder and redder. This was about to get ugly.

"Omigod! Shut up, you little psycho," Teagan muttered, glaring at Gary. If only she could actually defend her younger self. The more upset little Teagan got, the more squeamish older Teagan became.

"Why not?" Emily asked. "Why don't you want to play?"

"'Cuz it's a stupid game!" little Teagan shouted finally, whirling on her best friend. "I don't even know why you want to play it! It was a stupid, dumb idea!"

"Teagan!" Emily's mother said in a scolding voice. "Apologize."

Little Teagan turned on Mrs. Zeller. "You can't tell me what to do! This is my house and you're not my mother!"

Mrs. Zeller paled and looked at her husband like she was hoping for reinforcements. Unfortunately he looked even more uncomfortable than she did.

"Come on, Teagan. It's our birthday," Emily said quietly. Suddenly her face brightened. "What do *you* want to do? Whatever you want, we'll do it," she offered.

"I want you to leave me alone!" little Teagan shouted, pushing her heavy chair away from the table.

"I want you to leave me alone!" Gary repeated in a whiny voice.

"Shut up!" Little Teagan screamed in his face. "Shut up! Shut up! Shut up!"

Gary's maw of a mouth finally slapped closed.

As little Teagan raced past the door to the kitchen, Marcia returned with plates full of cake. Little Teagan paused for a split second and batted a few plates out of Marcia's hands with a *whack,* sending icing and plastic forks flying.

Teagan gasped. "I can't believe I just did that!"

A piece of cake hit the floor with a splat and another landed right on Jennifer's head. Jennifer instantly started to wail. Little Teagan ran out of the room and headed for the stairs as Marcia apologized like crazy and started cleaning up the mess. Mrs. Zeller tended to a hysterical Jennifer and Emily just sat there, looking for all the world like she had just lost her best friend.

"What's wrong with me?" Teagan asked. "How could I do that to Marcia?"

"You let your anger get the best of you," the ghost said. "As usual."

Teagan chose to ignore the tagline. "But why? Emily said I could do whatever I wanted. Usually that's my favorite thing to hear," Teagan said. "It's like I didn't even *want* to cheer up."

"Are you any different today?" the ghost asked, turning to face Teagan and looking her directly in the eye.

As Emily got up and started handing out the non-ruined pieces of cake to her friends, Teagan felt her blood start to boil.

"You know what, ghost?" she said. "You are getting on my last nerve."

"Too bad," the ghost said, taking Teagan's hand. "We're not done yet."

Interview with Teagan Phillips re:
Upcoming Sweet Sixteen Party
Transcript 4

Reporter: Melissa Bradshaw, Senior Editor,
Rosewood Prep Sentinel

MB: This is Melissa Bradshaw, back with Teagan Phillips to talk about her upcoming high-fashion sweet sixteen. Teagan, it's nice to see you again.

TP: Well, that other reporter turned out to be completely unprofessional.

MB: What exactly happened between you two? He won't talk to anyone on the staff and he's decided to just do box scores from now on. Says it's his calling or something. Do you know how boring box scores are?

TP: Well, we all have to follow our bliss. Do you have any actual questions for me?

MB: Right, well, I wanted to ask you what you hope to gain from this party.

TP: What I hope to gain?

MB: Yes, you're putting in all this effort and money and you're a smart girl on her way up in the world.

TP: Thank you for noticing.

MB: So you must want something good to come out of it. Prestige, popularity . . . .

TP: Are you suggesting I need to throw a party to get friends? Because I already have friends. Plenty of them. It's not like I need to bribe people to hang out with me.

MB: No. Of course not. I'm not suggesting that at all. I was just asking—

TP: What do I want to get out of this party? Well, a fun night and a ton of presents. How's that for an answer?

MB: Good enough. Good enough. Moving on . . .

Chapter 11

Teagan found herself standing on a tree-lined street, the sun warming her shoulders. Tiny, cookie-cutter houses stood all in a row, each a different color than the last, but each the exact same shape and design. Kids played hopscotch on the sidewalk and the driveways were filled with low-end cars like Hyundais and old-model Hondas. Everything looked very familiar, but Teagan couldn't put her finger on why. It wasn't like anyone she knew lived in a neighborhood like this. There were no gates, no winding driveways, no huge trees blocking out any and all views of the tremendous houses.

"Where are we?" she asked the ghost, taking a deep breath of the floral air. She pulled her Michael Kors sunglasses out of her bag and slipped them on.

The ghost took hold of Teagan's shoulders and turned her around. Everything came back to Teagan in a rush. Emily's house. Seeing the outside now was just as strange as standing in the entryway had been. There was the fading blue paint and the black shutters that didn't close. There was Mrs. Zeller's ugly black Ford Taurus in the driveway. There was the gap in the white picket fence where Gary had smashed through on his skateboard, ending up with thirty-four stitches in his leg—all because he was trying to impress Teagan with his skills. (Instead Teagan had fainted at the sight of all that blood.) There was the tulip border that she and Emily had helped plant when they were in grade school. And at the window, staring out at the street with a forlorn expression, was Emily herself.

Emily looked older than she had at their twelfth birthday party but younger than at her sixteenth. Her long blond hair was pulled back in a ponytail and her style had improved since age twelve. She was wearing a light pink tee with a screened-on surfer design and low-rise jeans. Probably sale items at Old Navy, but still a major upgrade from the awful corduroys.

"What year is this?" Teagan asked, taking a couple of steps toward the front walk.

Teagan felt a hand on her shoulder, and for a split second she thought they were outta there, but instead she suddenly found herself inside the house, standing right next to Emily. The floor below her feet trembled from the din of the party raging in the basement below. Music and laughter filled the house, but Emily looked to be in a decidedly party-pooping place. Her arms were crossed over her stomach. In one hand she held a small wrapped gift.

"What's she doing?" Teagan asked. "What kind of birthday girl ditches her own party?"

"You haven't been at yours for quite some time," the ghost said.

"Yeah? And whose fault is that?" Teagan tossed over her shoulder.

"Yours, actually," the ghost said. "You're the one who fell down the stairs."

"Hello? I'm dead over here!" Teagan trilled, waggling her fingers. "A little compassion, please?"

"Hey! I'm dead too!" the ghost told her.

Teagan blinked. "Oh yeah. Right."

A car approached out on the street and Emily jumped, leaning forward to see out the side of the window. Teagan could practically feel the sizzle of excitement coming off her. When she saw it was just a silver Acura, she clucked her tongue and resumed her former pose. It was all kind of . . . sad. It made Teagan think of the many, *many* times she had window-watched over the years, hoping her father would show.

"Who's she waiting for?" Teagan asked.

Feet pounded on the rickety basement stairs and the noise exploded for a second as the door opened and closed. Emily checked her plastic watch and sighed as Gary came barreling into the room.

"Whoa. Talk about an awkward phase," Teagan said with a smirk.

At about sixteen years of age, Gary was at least six-foot four and pushing 250 pounds. His red T-shirt strained to cover his rolls and his skin was covered with angry red pimples. How had he gone from this to the hottie who had appeared at Emily's sweet sixteen?

"I can't believe he actually let himself get like that," Teagan said. "But thank the Lord he turned it around."

The ghost cast her eyes heavenward. "Do you think you could focus on something beyond looks for five seconds?" she asked, opening her hands in frustration.

"What? I'm just *saying*," Teagan replied. "Jeez, ghost. Chill."

"Dude, what're you doing up here?" Gary asked Emily, out of breath. "Everyone's wondering where you are."

"She said she'd come," Emily half whined, turning away from the window for less than a second. "Where is she?"

"The girl is a total beyotch if she doesn't want to be here for your birthday," Gary said, doing a little downward hand gesture move that he probably thought was gangsta cool. It just made him look even dorkier. "But hello? There's like twenty-some people down there who *did* show."

"Yeah, but she said she'd come . . ." Emily said reluctantly.

Teagan swallowed down a hard lump that had formed in her throat.

"They're talking about me, aren't they?" she asked the ghost. "Where was I?"

The ghost took Teagan's hand, and in a rush of warm air, Emily was gone. The last thing Teagan saw was her former best friend tossing the tiny wrapped present on the couch. The card attached had one word scribbled across the front. *Teagan.* Next to it was a little *bff*.

Teagan brought her hands to her head in an attempt to quell the dizziness. She knew where she was before she even opened her eyes. The juniors department at Neiman Marcus had a very distinctive smell. Trendy perfume meets synthetic fabric meets recycled air. She would know it anywhere.

"I was at the *mall?*" Teagan asked, opening her eyes. The room spun and she leaned one hand on a table stacked with colorful silk T-shirts in an attempt to steady herself.

"I don't know why you should be surprised. You do spend

about eighty-five percent of your time here," the ghost said. She picked up a checkered cabbie hat and tried it on, turning to a small mirror and adjusting pieces of hair around her face.

"That's a gratuitous estimate," Teagan said, irritated. "I do have school."

"I meant eighty-five percent of your *free* time," the ghost said, discarding the hat.

Teagan blinked. "Oh."

Just then she heard her own voice babbling away over by the bathing suit display. Sure enough, there was Teagan, age fourteen, flanked by Lindsee, Ashley, and Maya. Ashley was pudgy and short, her teeth dotted with clear braces. Maya's dark hair was pulled back from her face with a headband, and without her now-size-D chest she looked significantly younger. Lindsee looked almost exactly the same but with slightly less makeup. Teagan, her arms full of clothing, was very skinny and self-assured. Teagan couldn't help smiling over the massive improvements she'd gone through since she was twelve. It just showed what a girl could accomplish when she put her mind to it. And stopped eating. And read nothing but beauty and fashion mags. And had a lot of free time on her hands.

"Here. Ring it up," young Teagan said, tossing at least three dozen hangers on the glass counter. The saleslady's eyes lit up and she dropped the copy of *Elle* she was perusing. Clearly she was foreseeing a nice fat commission for doing absolutely nothing. "You are going to look so hot in that pleated mini," young Teagan said to Lindsee.

"You don't *have* to buy it for me," Lindsee said, absently twirling her hair.

"Please! It would be a crime to leave it here," young Teagan replied.

"Omigod! Look at these cell phone cozies!" Lindsee squealed, picking a zebra-print sleeve off a rack on the counter.

"How cute are those?" Teagan said with a gasp. She removed a furry one with a leopard print and ran her fingers across it. "I *have* to have one."

"Excuse me! Are these real fur?" Maya asked, taking a brown one that looked like it was made out of mink.

"Of course not," the woman said with a snort as she removed an anti-theft tag from a pink leather jacket that Teagan had no recollection of ever wearing. "The whole line was personally approved by Alicia Silverstone herself."

"You're kidding," Ashley said, grabbing a model that looked like it was skinned from a dalmatian.

"I'm totally getting this," Teagan said, tossing it on top of the pile of clothing.

"Teagan! It's a hundred dollars," Ashley gasped, checking the price tag.

"So?" young Teagan said. She whipped a credit card out of her wallet. "It's on Daddy."

"You are *so* bad!" Lindsee said.

"Wanna see bad? Here." Young Teagan grabbed all three cell phone cozies out of their hands and dumped them on the counter. "Gifts for my friends," she told the saleslady with a smile.

"Teagan! Don't!" Maya protested halfheartedly as she eyed the cozy with a certain lust in her eyes.

"Please! It's my birthday and I want to do something nice for my friends," young Teagan said. "Besides, we *have* to have these. Everyone at school is going to lust after them."

"Your dad is going to kill you!" Lindsee said gleefully.

"Like he'll ever even notice," young Teagan said.

"We used those things for about a week," Teagan told the ghost with a shudder. "So gauche."

"Four hundred dollars' worth of gauche," the ghost said flatly. "Plus tax."

As the saleslady went about busily scanning, folding, and packing, young Teagan surreptitiously checked her watch. Teagan saw her younger self bite her bottom lip. Then, the moment she noticed Lindsee watching her, she glanced away and tossed back her hair.

"Oh yeah," Lindsee said, sliding toward Teagan at the counter. "Don't you have that lame-ass party to go to this afternoon?"

Young Teagan threw off a blithe little laugh. "Lindsee! Please! We haven't even hit the shoe department yet!"

Okay, I totally suck, Teagan thought, picturing Emily standing at that window.

The saleslady announced Teagan's total—over three thousand dollars—and young Teagan slapped the credit card down without pause. She signed the receipt with a flourish and her friends helped her tote away her many bags. Teagan and the ghost followed them out of the department store and into the bright and shiny mall.

"You know what we should do?" Ashley said, her eyes bright. "We should hit the new Häagen-Dazs! I'm starving."

Young Teagan put her hand over her flat stomach. "God, Ashley! I've already had, like, three hundred calories today! Make me yak!"

"I need to sit down," Teagan said, dragging herself toward a bench at the edge of the food court. She dropped her purse on the floor and slumped, her legs splayed out in front of her. Yet another perk of being invisible. There was no way in hell she would ever strike this particular pose in public.

"What's the matter, Teagan?" the ghost asked, sitting down next to her and primly crossing her legs at the ankle.

"What's the matter!?" Teagan flipped up her head, her hair cascading down her back. Major head rush. She squeezed her eyes shut until it passed. "Did you not *see* that?" she blurted, holding her forehead in her hand. "I'm awful! I mean, did you see how depressed Emily was? I couldn't have just gone over there for an hour even? What was wrong with me?"

"You had moved on. Just not to better things," the ghost said patiently. "You wanted Lindsee and the others to be your friends from the moment you stepped through the doors at Rosewood. This day, you found a way to make that happen."

"What do you—"

Teagan stared at the ghost as she suddenly remembered. She remembered calling Lindsee that morning and asking her to go shopping. She remembered how Lindsee had said she had other plans with Ashley and Maya. She remembered the panic that had set in at the idea of being rejected. She remembered telling Lindsee that she had her father's credit card— how she had implied that they could all use it. Half an hour later, Lindsee, Maya, and Ashley had all shown up at her door, ready to go. Had she really bought her current friends? Would any of them be hanging out with her today if not for that shopping spree?

How could the ghost *know* about all this?

The ghost took a deep breath of the greasy, salty air, sitting up straight and closing her eyes. "Dear God, it's been a long time since I've had a cheeseburger," she said, letting it out.

Teagan's stomach groaned. "Tell me about it," she mumbled, feeling light-headed.

"So. You ready for your next stop?" the ghost asked.

"Not really," Teagan replied, slumping lower.

"Too bad!" the ghost said perkily. She threw her arm over Teagan's shoulders and then they were off.

Rosewood Prep Sentinel

GOSSIP PAGE

Weekly Poll
By Laura Wood, Senior Writer

This week, we asked one hundred students what they would be getting sophomore and it girl of the moment Teagan Phillips for her birthday. Hate to spoil the surprises, Teagan, but some of these we just had to print.

Janice Bennet, junior: I'm thinking three Shelli Segal dresses, all the same style but different sizes. That way if she drops some of the baby fat or, you know, bloats up, she'll still be able to fit into at least one of them.

Tyler Rascoe, sophomore: I already put in my order at Trashy Lingerie. The whip should be arriving any day now.

Christian Alexi, sophomore: American Express gift cards. That way if they get stolen, no one else can use them. They're the gift of the responsible consumer.

Viola Fellini, senior: Ugh. As a senior, I think I should be exempt from attending sweet sixteens.

Shari Marx, sophomore: She gave me a gift certificate for a makeover. I might give her a gift certificate for a gym.

Max Modell, sophomore: I haven't decided yet. Maybe a framed picture of my new head shot?

Maya Reynolds and Ashley Harrison: We can't tell you! It's a surprise! But it's gonna be *really* good.

Chapter 12

"Aw yeah, baby! It's getting hot in here now!" Shay shouted into his microphone, raising one hand into the air.

Teagan whirled around. She was back in the center of her sweet sixteen. The dance floor was slamming with people and apparently, Shay had decided to keep up with the cheesy DJ act.

If I were alive, I would totally stop payment on his check, Teagan thought. But she didn't dwell too long. Finally she had her chance to check out the scene she had worked so hard to create. She stepped to the side of the dance floor to take it all in.

All around the room, models posed on their personal stages, looking bored. Teagan saw Trey Duncan trying to talk to one of them—Bonnie, if memory served—but the girl, adhering to her instructions for the night, ignored him. Teagan had been very specific with her directives to the models. They were there to pose and to show off her clothes. No fraternizing. Couldn't blame Trey, though. Bonnie did look

hot in Teagan's black mini flapper-esque design with the feath-
ers at the bustline. Even in the insanity, Teagan couldn't help
but admire her own design.

"Nice one," the ghost said, following her gaze. "You're
good."

"I know," Teagan said. Then she saw the ghost's disapprov-
ing glance and rolled her eyes. "I mean, thank you. God. Is it
so bad to have self-confidence?"

"Self-confidence is one thing. Major ego is another."

"All right. All right," Teagan said, waving her hand.

Everyone on the dance floor was gathered around in a hap-
hazard circle, watching somebody get down in the center as
they clapped along to the beat. Unbelievable. It was like no one
had even noticed she was gone. Hello? Whose party *was* this?

Shari Marx scurried toward the crowd in her Jimmy
Choos and before Teagan could get out of the way, Shari slid
right through her.

Every inch of her body exploded with white-hot pain. Her
eyes burst. Her heart stopped. Her skin sizzled and burned
right off, leaving only charred bone. Teagan staggered backward into the ghost's arms, screaming in panic.

Oh God! This *is death!* Teagan thought wildly, sweat pouring from her skin. *Shari Marx just killed me all over again.*

Her eyes rolled wildly and somewhere her brain registered
that she had not, in fact, been incinerated. She could still see
her body intact; she just couldn't make herself believe that she
had survived a sensation like that. Desperate, Teagan tried to
suck in some air, but her lungs wouldn't respond.

"Calm down, Teagan. Just breathe," the ghost said, patting
her on the back. "You're still here. Sort of."

Suddenly Teagan's chest expanded as her throat and lungs

filled with air. She coughed and staggered toward a deserted corner of the floor.

"What was that?" she asked, holding her hand to her chest. Gradually the heat started to fade, leaving her skin humming.

"I know. Freaky, right?" the ghost said, pulling a face.

Teagan shot her a patented look of death, but then a huge cheer went up on the dance floor, distracting her from the homicide at hand.

"What's going on over there?" she asked, forcing herself to stand up straight. Breathe in, breathe out. Breathe in, breathe out.

"I don't know. Why don't you go find out?" the ghost asked.

"Oh no," Teagan said. "I am not walking through all those bodies. No way."

The ghost rolled her eyes. "Wuss."

She slapped her hand on Teagan's shoulder and they instantly reappeared in the center of the circle. Teagan's jaw dropped when she saw the scene that had captured everyone's attention. Lindsee and Max were getting it on right in the center of the circle. Her hips ground against his as they lowered themselves toward the floor and back up again. Lindsee threw her arms in the air and swung her head back and forth, shimmying away like the second coming of Xtina. She turned around and bent over, rubbing her butt up against Max's midsection. All the guys in the crowd cheered and whistled. It was like something out of Skinamax.

"Omigod. Get me a hose," Teagan said. She glared around at her so-called friends. "Doesn't anyone here care that he's *my* boyfriend? Hello? It's *my* sweet sixteen! Shouldn't *I* be out there with him?"

"Damn. That girl can drop it like it's hot," the ghost said.

"Oh, please. Do not try to sound hip. You're just embarrassing yourself," Teagan said. "Why the hell did you bring me here? Do I *really* need to see this?"

"I thought you *wanted* to check in on your ultimate creation," the ghost reminded her.

Melissa Bradshaw, reporter extraordinaire, circled the couple with her camera out, grinning as she snapped away. Not only was everyone Teagan knew witnessing this spectacle, but come Wednesday morning, when the new *Sentinel* was released, they would all have full-color photos to remember it by.

Of course, the article would probably be accompanied by her obituary, so maybe it was actually all relative.

"To tell you the truth, I just wanted to see how the Maya-Ashley fashion show was playing out," the ghost said. Then she grinned. "Ah! There's Maya now!"

Teagan glanced across the circle and saw Maya emerge with a curious expression. She was wearing a tasteful black bias-cut dress with a one-shoulder top. Teagan had seen her in it a hundred times, but she had to admit her friend wore it well. Maya caught a glimpse of the disgusting display on the dance floor and stalked right into the center of the circle.

"Lindsee! What the hell are you doing?" Maya demanded, grabbing Lindsee's arm and yanking her away from Max.

Teagan was stunned. She had never seen Maya talk back to Lindsee about anything. Ever. Let alone confront her first.

"Dancing. God! What's your problem?" Lindsee asked as Max continued to try to dry-hump her side.

"What about Teagan?" Maya demanded. "This is her party and you're slobbering all over her man!"

"Ooooh!" a few members of the crowd chorused.

"Nice!" Teagan cheered.

"Dial it down a notch, Maya," Max told her, looping his arm around Lindsee's waist. "You're gonna shatter glass."

"Besides, no one's even seen Teagan in, like, half an hour," Lindsee said with a shrug. "She's probably busy looking in a mirror somewhere."

"Ugh!" Teagan shouted. "You backstabbing bitch!"

Maya looked like she was about to blow, but obviously trying to get through to Lindsee and Max was pointless. It was clear that they only had eyes for each other from that moment on. Maya whirled around indignantly and her jaw dropped. Following her gaze, Teagan and the ghost turned to find Ashley, having just elbowed her way to the center of the circle, wearing not the same dress as Maya but one that was damn similar. Black. Skimpy. Strap on the opposite shoulder.

The ghost cracked up laughing. "What is *with* these girls?"

Teagan watched in dismay as both Maya and Ashley turned around and smashed their way back through the crowd.

"You guys! It's not the same dress!" Teagan shouted, but it didn't matter. They couldn't have heard her over the music if she had actually been there.

"I don't believe it," Teagan said finally, turning to the ghost. "I can't believe Maya actually defended me against Lindsee."

"Sometimes it takes a crap situation to find out who your real friends are," the ghost said. "You know, like death."

"But I practically ignored her," Teagan said, letting the ghost's lame joke slide by. "And Lindsee and I picked on her and Ashley behind their backs all the time."

"Yeah. Maybe you shouldn't have done that," the ghost said,

patting Teagan on the back. "Maya may be kind of vain and a bit of a follower, but she's a good person. And Ashley's the one who came up with the idea for that killer present they made for you. Which, by the way, did take them weeks to put together."

"Really?"

"Yep. And then you completely forgot about it the second you saw they were wearing the same thing and realized they *might* put a minor cramp in your big night," the ghost said. "Really nice."

"Oh God. Ashley even called me to sing 'Happy Birthday' this morning and I totally blew her off!" Teagan said, covering her face with her hands. "You're right. They *are* good friends."

The ghost nodded. "Lindsee, on the other hand . . ."

She trailed off as she looked back toward the Lindsee-and-Max Show, which was getting hotter and heavier by the second.

"I can't take it anymore." Teagan shook her head. Two feet away, Max pulled a very willing Shari toward him and made himself the meat in a Shari and Lindsee sandwich. "Do we have to be here?"

"Thought you'd never ask," the ghost said.

She took Teagan's arm and whisked her away.

Teagan rematerialized in Emily's living room again, but this time the atmosphere was much more subdued. Glancing around, she saw that she was back at Emily's house and that the place was packed with people in full-on black. Black dresses, black suits, black shirts, black bags. Emily's dad talked with a priest near the window, whispering and nodding. A pair of middle-aged women in the corner hugged as one of them dabbed at her eyes with a handkerchief. Emily's mother walked in from the kitchen, her face wet with tears, and placed a tray of cookies in the center of the coffee table. Everyone whispered and followed Mrs. Zeller with their eyes.

"What's going on? Who died?" Teagan asked.

The ghost clucked her tongue and shook her head.

"What? It's a valid question," Teagan said. "What happened?"

Then her eyes fell on Emily and for a moment, Teagan couldn't speak. Emily looked . . . old. Not wrinkled and sun-spotted old, but older. Any baby fat had fallen away from her face, leaving high cheekbones and bright eyes. Her hair was pulled back in a bun and she was wearing a flattering black pantsuit. She looked pretty. Sophisticated. And very, very sad.

"Is this the . . . the future?" Teagan asked, her knees feeling weak.

"Yep," the ghost said. "Six years ahead, to be exact."

"Wow. Wicked," Teagan said. Then her heart skipped a beat as she recalled how freaky it had been to see her twelve-year-old self. "Am I here? What do I look like?"

The ghost rolled her eyes. "Just focus, would you?"

Gary walked into the room, wearing a suit and looking much like he had in the last visit but with shorter hair. He sat down next to his sister on the couch, dropped his arm around her shoulders, and gave her a squeeze.

"This is my fault," Emily said, staring straight ahead. "I should have been here. I would have been able to help."

"Emily, come on," Gary said, his voice soothing. "What were you going to do? Not go to college? What would that have solved?"

"I could have helped her!" Emily said, raising her voice. "I would have done something!"

The already-hushed room fell eerily silent. Emily noticed everyone staring at her and looked at her lap, trying hard not to cry. Gary pulled her to him and she leaned her head on his shoulder, the tears dripping silently down her face and wetting the lapel of his jacket.

Teagan noticed a kid of about twelve at the other end of the couch, his foot bouncing up and down as he stared stoically into space. His brown hair was mussed and his shirt was two sizes too big. He wore a red tie that was so short it looked like it had been bought for an eight-year-old's first communion.

"Ricky? Do you want anything to eat?" Mrs. Zeller asked him, leaning in.

"No. Leave me alone," Ricky said, his voice thick.

Teagan knew that voice. She knew that tone. That had been *her* once. Right after her mother had died—she had sounded just like that. It was all she needed to hear to understand, finally, what was going on. It hit her with the force of a wrecking ball and she gasped, backing into the wall. That was little Ricky at the end of the couch. This was Catherine's funeral. Emily's aunt Catherine. Ricky's mother was dead.

"Oh my God," Teagan said.

"Ricky? Come on, honey, I know you're upset, but you have to eat," Mrs. Zeller said, reaching for his knee.

Ricky jumped out of his chair like he'd just been hit with a hot poker. "I said leave me alone!" he screeched, anger spewing from his every pore.

He turned and ran out of the house, slamming the door so hard the walls shook. Teagan felt every single ounce of his pain. Suddenly it was as if her mother had died all over again. She experienced the anger, the confusion, the utter, hollowing loss like it was yesterday.

"I'll go," Gary said, pushing himself up. Emily leaned her elbow on the arm of the couch, sniffling hard.

"What happened?" Teagan asked, holding her hand over her stomach. "How did she die?"

"She overdosed," the ghost said, her eyes rimmed with red. "She had been in and out of programs for the past few years, but nothing worked. Ricky came home from school and found her in the bathroom."

"How awful," Teagan said, covering her mouth now. Her stomach convulsed and she tasted bile in the back of her mouth. She swallowed and her throat burned, bringing tears to her eyes.

She took a deep breath and tried to steady herself. Mrs. Zeller buried her face in her husband's chest and the guests all shifted uncomfortably, unsure of what to do. Teagan had to turn her back to the room.

"This is all because I got her fired?" she asked finally. "Is that why you're showing me this?"

The ghost sighed. "She was supposed to be promoted to banquet manager the night of your party," she said, clasping her hands behind her back. "She would have had a raise and benefits. Instead she ended up taking a series of crappy jobs, working twenty-four/seven to make ends meet and pay off her debts. She fell into a deep depression and started using again. Since she never had insurance, she couldn't afford any decent detox programs. Unfortunately there's very little recourse for people like Catherine. From the moment of her firing, she was a lost cause."

Teagan struggled for breath as she watched her former best friend dissolve in a fresh wave of guilt-ridden tears. Emily thought this was all her fault, but really it was Teagan's. The girl was going to walk around with that weight on her shoulders for the rest of her life and she had Teagan to thank for it. And poor Ricky. Teagan knew what it felt like to lose a mother. It didn't matter how it happened. It didn't matter when. His life was never going to be the same.

"I had no idea," Teagan said, her words choppy. "I . . . I didn't know. I . . . did . . . didn't think—"

"Well, that's the problem," the ghost said, taking Teagan's hand gently. "You never did."

Interview with Teagan Phillips re:
Upcoming Sweet Sixteen Party
Transcript 4, cont'd.

Reporter: Melissa Bradshaw, Senior Editor,
Rosewood Prep Sentinel

MB: So what time does the party of the century start?

TP: Eight o'clock. And we have the ballroom until one, but I'm sure we'll go longer than that.

MB: I'm sure. What's the extra two thousand dollars an hour you have to throw at them to keep the place open?

TP: Exactly! Well, Missy, you've done your research.

MB: I do like to know my beat.

TP: Anyway, you can bet I'll be the last one there. Well, me and Max and Lindsee and the rest of my crew. We know how to party.

MB: I don't doubt it.

TP: After the country club we'll probably even take the action back to my house. Believe me, this is going to be one night that no one will want to see end.

Chapter 13

Suddenly Teagan felt hardwood floor beneath her feet. She glanced dully around the country club ballroom. Things had calmed down quite a bit. Shay was nowhere to be seen and had left some unobtrusive R&B tune on low volume. Guests were taking their seats at the tables, tucking chiffon trains beneath their backsides and unfolding linen napkins. The waiters moved about silently, placing plates heaped with filet mignon or salmon in front of the delighted diners. Teagan found herself wondering which table Emily's aunt Catherine would have been assigned to. If Teagan hadn't lost control, would Catherine be smiling and chatting with her fellow waiters like that brunette chick across the room right now? Would she be looking forward to a bright future instead of one where she died young and left her son parentless? Just thinking about it exhausted Teagan. It was difficult, thinking about other people.

"Do we really have to be here now?" she asked the ghost.

Her shoulders slumped. "I don't really care if people are impressed anymore."

"Actually, right now, we do need to be here," the ghost replied.

Teagan managed to lift her eyes and check the table where she was supposed to be sitting with Max, Lindsee, Maya, Ashley, and the guys. No one was there but Marco and Christian, who were tearing into the garlic ciabatta rolls like starving street dogs and spewing crumbs everywhere. No one seemed even to notice that the guest of honor was MIA.

"You know what? Screw you," Teagan said finally. "I'm sick of this."

She started across the room, gripping her purse with both hands. As she wove her way around the tables, she carefully avoided any and all human contact.

"Where do you think you're going?" the ghost called after her.

"I don't know! Somewhere away from you!" she shouted back defiantly.

She was almost free when she caught a glimpse of her father, slumped back in a chair near the wall. He and Karen were conversing over a small table filled with half-empty used glasses. Karen had pulled her chair around to Teagan's father's side so that she could hold his hand. Teagan had never seen her father look this distraught. At least not outside one of these freaky flashbacks she'd been dragged through tonight.

"It's all my fault," he said, staring down at his fiancée's hands. "I spoiled her too much."

Teagan's heart thumped extra hard and she took a tentative step toward the couple. She wasn't entirely sure she wanted to hear this, but it was next to impossible to resist.

"Michael, don't be so hard on yourself," Karen said, reaching up to touch his cheek. Her thumb caressed his skin, and Teagan was shocked to find that she wasn't completely skeeved by the parental PDA.

"Who else is there to blame?" Teagan's father asked, his eyes wide. "She's my daughter. I'm responsible for her. What have I been doing all this time?"

Karen leaned in a bit farther and their knees touched. "You've done what any loving father would do," Karen said firmly, looking him in the eye. "You've given your daughter the best of everything."

"Except me," Teagan's father said sorrowfully. "I haven't given her the best of me."

Holy crap. He did not just say that, Teagan thought.

Her heart ached and a single tear spilled over down her cheek. She couldn't believe it. He got it. He actually got that he had never been there. All this time she had thought that he was so clueless—that he had no idea—that he had forgotten she existed. Now all she wanted to do was shout in relief. Every ounce of longing and resentment she had ever felt had just been validated. But at the same time, she was struck with an incredible urge to hug him and tell him that it was okay. That it was fine. That he wasn't an awful father. Just looking at him so upset, so broken made her feel like maybe she had overreacted to everything that had ever happened between her and him. Was this all she had ever needed? A little acknowledgment? A few stupid words?

At that moment she loved him like she had never loved anyone before. All because he had shown a chink in the armor.

Teagan's father took a deep breath and sat up straight, shaking his head. He leaned forward as well and blew out a sigh. "After Lauren died, I just didn't know how to be close to her," he said. "She reminded me so much of her mother. It was so hard."

"Of course it was," Karen said without missing a beat. It clearly didn't bother her to be talking about her man's former wife. Teagan could tell from the look on Karen's face that all the woman cared about right then was being there for her fiancé.

"I pulled away. I can see that now," her father said, on a roll. "I gave her *things* instead of hugs. I apologized with gifts. I was never there. I just . . . I wish I could go back."

There was no controlling anything now. Teagan burst into sobs, crying openly, letting the tears spill freely over her face. It was liberating, really, not trying to hold it in. Not choking it back. She had spent so many years forcing herself not to cry that she never realized how incredible it actually felt to let it go.

Her father did love her. He really did.

The ghost came up behind Teagan and handed her a napkin. Teagan wiped her entire face with it, coming away with huge smudges of mascara and eyeliner, base and blush. All Sophia Killen's hard work, washed away like that. Teagan laughed through her tears, imagining how horrifying she must look right then. Being invisible really did have its perks.

"You're a wreck," the ghost said.

"Who cares? Did you hear that?" Teagan replied, smiling.

"Sure did," the ghost replied, looking satisfied.

Teagan watched her father as he took a deep breath, his head bowed to the ground. What she wouldn't give just then to have her body back. She had no idea what she would say to him, but whatever it was, it would be perfect.

Then her father lifted his eyes and said, "I feel like I failed Lauren."

Teagan's breath caught in her throat and her tears were brought up short. "What? No!" She walked over to stand next to the table, panic welling up inside her. "Dad, no."

"Of course you haven't," Karen said.

"See! Listen to Karen!" Teagan said.

"I have," her father replied. "Our daughter is so beautiful on the outside, but I have no idea who she is on the inside. Who is that girl who screamed at that waitress? Who screamed at me? Who walked out on her own party and went God knows where without even letting us know? What goes on inside her head? What kind of person *is* she?"

"Omigod, he thinks I'm awful," Teagan said, her skin prickling with heat. "I'm not a horrible person, Dad. I'm not. Come on! It's a . . . a high-stress night! I'm not evil! I mean, I didn't know! I didn't know that she needed the job so much. I—"

"They can't hear you, Teagan," the ghost said.

Teagan whirled around, her vision blurry. "But I have to tell him! I don't want him to think he raised some monster. I don't want him to think Mom hates him. It's not his fault. It's . . ."

Teagan heard what she was saying and snapped her mouth shut. The ghost eyed her expectantly, but the condescension in her expression just made Teagan's toes curl. She wasn't going to say what the ghost wanted her to say. She wasn't going to say this was all on her.

Taking a deep breath, Teagan wiped under her eyes and composed herself. She couldn't believe she had cried like that in front of this stupid ghost. She couldn't believe she had let herself go that far. Enough was enough.

"I can't take this anymore," she said stoically. "You and me? We're done."

Then she turned on her heel and stalked back through the

room. She had no idea where she was going. All she knew was that she had to put as much distance as possible between herself and her father. There was no way she could listen to him anymore — hear his disappointment — and know that there was absolutely nothing she could do to make it up to him. She was dead. She was dead and her father was going to find out soon and he was always going to think that she was some tremendously heartless spoiled brat. And he was always going to think it was his fault.

But I'm not horrible. I'm not, Teagan told herself, trying to keep from losing it completely.

She was a straight-A student. She was one of the most popular girls in her class. Her future would have been bright and full of possibilities. Just look at the incredible party she had pulled together. Look at her designs! With her exquisite taste, her talent, and her organizational abilities, she could have been a world-famous designer. She could have been a party planner to the stars! Editor in chief of a major fashion magazine! She could have done anything she wanted. If, of course, she were still alive.

The ghost could kiss it.

Teagan headed for the first door she saw and shoved her way through it, chin lifted in defiance. She stopped the second she realized she had stalked purposefully into the kitchen. Steam from the stove tops assaulted her and the clanging of the pots and pans jangled her already-raw nerves. Half a dozen chefs and kitchen workers raced about, cooking and cleaning, shouting to one another, and creating an ever-moving obstacle between Teagan and the back door.

The last thing she wanted to do was mistakenly walk through one of *these* guys.

Then Shay stepped out from behind a tall shelf, carrying a few empty aluminum trays. What the hell was he doing back here?

"Yo! Pack up some of those eggplant mozzarella rolls!" Shay called out to one of the busboys. "And you got any extra bread?"

"Absolutely, man," a guy in a stained white apron replied. "You know, I was listening to your stuff out there. You're not bad."

"Thanks," Shay said.

"I do a little spinning myself," the busboy told him.

"Where? His grandmother's basement?" Teagan grumbled.

"Yeah? You any good?" Shay asked.

"Could show you a thing or two," the kid said, pulling his shirt away from his skin like he was too cool, then laughing.

Shay slapped his shoulder. "You should come out later. Show me what you got for a coupla tracks."

"Seriously?" the kid asked.

"Seriously."

"Oh, perfect! Let's have the busboy DJ my half-a-million-dollar party," Teagan cried. "Sounds like a plan!"

Together the two guys laid out the trays and loaded them up with leftover hors d'oeuvres from the cocktail hour.

"It's cool of you to do this," the kitchen worker told Shay, brushing his hands together as he reached for a platter full of raw veggies. "The people down at that shelter must love you."

Shay grinned and shrugged. "Everyone deserves a gourmet meal once in a while."

The ghost pushed through the door behind Teagan, who was standing there in indignant shock. "He's going to let that busboy over there DJ the party," Teagan told the ghost. "And they're taking the hors d'oeuvres *I* paid for," she added, throwing out her hands. "Shay Beckford is *stealing* from me!"

"Everyone except the birthday girl," the busboy said with a laugh. "Did you see that chica's bony butt? Does she even eat?"

Shay laughed and Teagan turned ten shades of purple. "Okay, I draw the line at the help picking on me."

"He did say you have a bony butt, though," the ghost said. "I'd think you'd be pleased."

Inside, Teagan *was* pleased, a little. But still, where did these guys get off? They were taking food that rightfully belonged to Teagan and her guests. Not that anyone here would have ever gone home with doggie bags. That was way too gauche. But still, it was the principle of the thing.

"Did you check out the size of the haul she took in?" the busboy asked. "They actually hired a coupla security guys to watch over it all. Hey! Maybe you can get her to donate some of her presents."

"Yeah, right," Shay said with a scoff, adding a cardboard lid to his tray and sealing it up. "That girl would sooner part with her toenails than give up her swag."

"Ugh!" Teagan blurted, staring Shay down. She would have given anything to be able to smack him across his smug little face just then. "You don't know me!" she shouted. "You can't judge me, you little thief!"

Shay went about stacking the trays and bagging up a couple dozen rolls. Teagan was practically trembling with frustration. He was so self-righteous, the little Robin Hood. Taking from the rich to give to the poor. Showing off about it to his little friend. Like he wasn't going home to some fab loft stocked with every brand-new state-of-the-art electronic gadget and a giant Sony flat screen with Bose surround sound. Please.

"What is with everybody?" Teagan asked the ghost. "Why do they all think they know me so freakin' well? I can be a good person! I can be surprising!"

"All evidence to the contrary," the ghost said wryly.

"Hey! I gave that woman a fifty this morning, little miss I Know Everything!" Teagan said, whirling on the ghost. "Did ya know that?"

"But why did you do it?" the ghost asked. "Did you do it because you wanted to help, or did you do it because you felt guilty?"

Teagan blinked but quickly recovered. "Come on! Doesn't half the charitable giving in the world happen because of guilt?" she wailed in frustration. "At least I gave it to her! That has to count for something!"

"I better put these in the van," Shay said, picking up his trays. "I gotta get back out there and do my job."

"Damn straight you do," Teagan said.

"Yo, man. You should come back here after for the cake," the busboy said. "Not like any a' these Atkins-obsessed prisses are gonna eat it."

Shay laughed as he backed out the door to the parking lot, his arms full. "Will do. Thanks, man."

"Maybe I'll pay off those dudes and grab a couple of those presents for myself," the busboy added to himself as he dried his hands, laughing. "How many tiaras does one babe need?"

"Stay away from my gifts, you freak!" Teagan squealed.

The ghost laughed. "He's funny."

"You!" Teagan shouted, advancing on the ghost with one finger raised to the woman's bandaged chin. "This is all your fault! I should be . . . I don't know . . . hanging out with some angels on a cloud somewhere by now, and instead I'm trapped in this LSD trip from hell with *you*! Why are you doing this to me? Why couldn't you pick on someone else?"

The ghost looked steadily into Teagan's eyes. "Well, you've finally gotten one thing right," she said matter-of-factly. "This is all my fault."

Interview with Teagan Phillips re:
Upcoming Sweet Sixteen Party
Transcript 4, cont'd.

Reporter: Melissa Bradshaw, Senior Editor, *Rosewood Prep Sentinel*

MB: Let's dial it back a notch and talk a bit about sweet sixteens in general.

TP: Okay.

MB: Why do you think having a sweet sixteen is so important to girls today?

TP: Well, because it's like the one huge thing you have to look forward to. I mean, you can have a huge party every year, but a sweet sixteen is like an excuse to go all out. Not everyone gets to have a bat mitzvah, you know. And, like, what are the rest of us going to do—wait for our *weddings*? That could be *ages* from now.

MB: So you assume you'll have a wedding someday?

TP: Of course I will. Why wouldn't I?

MB: Well, some women choose not to get married. You know, the whole independent thing.

TP: Oh, well, that's not me. I mean, I want a

career, but when it comes to love, I'm more the traditional type.

(*laughter*)

TP: What?

MB: Oh! Just a (*coughing*) tickle in my throat!

TP: So I plan on finding true love and living the rest of my life with a guy who will pamper me and take me on lavish vacations and worship me forever.

MB: Sounds like you've got the perfect future.

TP: Without question.

Chapter 14

"Stop doing that!" Teagan shouted, ripping her arm out of the ghost's grip as she became solid again. "Haven't you ever heard of 'no means no'?"

"A ghost's gotta do what a ghost's gotta do," the woman replied blithely.

"Where the hell are we now?" Teagan asked. Then she finally took a second to look around. Her mouth fell open and she gasped. "Whoa. This place is gorgeous."

She was standing in the center of a huge loft apartment. Windows stretched from the gleaming blond wood floor all the way up to the ceiling two stories above, which was inlaid with intricate gold sheeting. A fireplace was built into an exposed brick wall, surrounded by plush white couches that were strewn with dozens of colorful throw pillows. Asymmetrical shelving lined the walls with pieces of modern pottery and blown glass set one to a shelf, like they were on display at a museum. Teagan stepped tentatively toward the windows and looked out across Central Park, in New York City. Down below, cabs lined up at a red light and joggers traversed the paths. Teagan salivated. This was exactly how she had always dreamed of living. If she had her checkbook on her, she would have whipped it out right then and made an offer.

"Where are we?" she asked, pulling the strap of her bag up on her shoulder as she turned to the ghost.

A door slammed and Teagan jumped.

"You already know what I want!" someone shouted, her voice echoing off the walls. "All you have to do now is say, 'Yes, miss. I'll see right to it,' and this conversation is officially over!"

The ghost sighed and sat down on a white leather bench as another woman stalked into the room, her high heels click clacking against the floor. She wore shiny white capri pants and a black tank top that clung to her scrawny frame. She lifted her head and tossed her hair back as she shouted at the top of her lungs. A vein in the center of her forehead bulged like it was fit to pop. Teagan recognized her instantly.

"Holy crap. That's you," Teagan said, her eyes wide. "This is *your* place?"

"Yep," the ghost said, pressing her hands into the bench at her sides. She looked tense. Like she would rather be any- where but here. Teagan had been experiencing that very sen- sation all night long.

"Who're you yelling at?" Teagan asked, looking around.

"Oh, that's my business manager," the ghost said.

"Where?"

"She's on the phone," the ghost said. "Oh yeah, right. In the future all you need is a little pod in your ear. You say the name of the person you want to call out loud and it connects you. You can imagine the confusion it causes on the streets."

"Wow," Teagan said as the woman continued to shout. She stormed right past them and into the kitchen at the far end of the apartment. "So you're, like, filthy rich."

"I was," the ghost said. "Come on."

The ghost got up and Teagan followed her into an immense kitchen. Modern appliances gleamed in the sunlight. The white tile was spotless. A glass bowl of ripe fruit sat in the center of a long glass table. Just looking at it made Teagan's stomach grumble.

"Unbelievable. I should fire that psycho," the woman said, ripping open the refrigerator door.

"Are you still on the phone?" Teagan asked.

"No. The call was terminated," the ghost said. "See what I mean about the confusion?"

The woman pulled out a nutrition bar of some kind and ripped open the brown wrapper. She stuffed the end of the bar in her mouth but had to wrench it back and forth before a piece finally tore off between her teeth. Teagan made a face. Whatever that thing was made out of, it didn't look appetizing. As the woman chewed—and chewed—and chewed some more, she powered up a tiny computer sitting on the counter.

The ghost walked behind her other self and gazed over her shoulder. Teagan followed. The woman was scrolling through her schedule.

Gym . . . full body wax . . . Anistoga class . . . massage . . . gym . . . Barneys w/Casey . . . gym.

"You sure work out a lot," Teagan said, impressed.

"Yeah. Kind of sucks that I died so young," the ghost joked, frowning. "All that work for nothing."

"What's Anistoga class?" Teagan asked.

"Oh, remember Jennifer Aniston?" the ghost said. "She

created this whole new yoga-pilates-aerobic fusion thing and made like a kabillion dollars selling DVDs and downloads."

"You're kidding."

"No. It's pretty huge," the ghost said.

Finally the woman stood up straight and swallowed. Teagan was disgusted to note that she had *just* finished her first and only bite of that bar. Apparently the diet snack industry hadn't come a long way.

"Call Dr. Jaber," the woman said.

"Here we go." The ghost took a deep breath and walked over to the kitchen table. She lowered herself into one of the high-backed chairs and leaned her head on her hand. Watching her other self pacing the room, she shook her head in wonder.

"What's going on?" Teagan asked.

"Just watch."

"Roseanne? I need to talk to Dr. Jaber," the woman said. "What? Oh, please. He's not at lunch and you know it. Tell him who it is!"

Teagan glanced at the ghost, her eyebrows raised. The ghost simply shrugged and rolled her eyes.

"Dr. Jaber. Yes, it is. Yes," the woman said. "I want to schedule another surgery," she said, reaching up to touch her chin. She looked at her reflection in a mirror set into the wall. "No. I'm not pleased with the results."

There was a moment of silence in which Teagan actually saw the color rise from the woman's neckline all the way up through her chin to her cheeks to her forehead.

"Wait a minute! Who the hell do you think you are? You're the one who screwed it up! You can't tell me not to—" Her eyes bulged as the doctor on the other end of the line spoke.

"I don't *care* if you think it's dangerous! I want it done and I want it done next week!"

The woman slammed her hands down on the counter, causing the cutlery inside a drawer to rattle.

"Look. Look! Hey! I'm talking here!" she shouted. "I am paying you, am I not? This is your job, is it not?" She waited a moment. "Good, then schedule it!"

The woman ripped a small black pod out of her ear and held it to her mouth. "Terminate call!" she screamed. Then she hurled the pod across the room, where it bounced against the window and rolled underneath a cabinet.

"Yeah, you don't have to throw it. You really just need to say 'terminate call,'" the ghost said, seeing Teagan's look of confusion.

Teagan blew out a breath and leaned back against the wall as the woman grabbed her nutrition bar and stalked out of the kitchen.

"No offense, ghost, but you were kind of a bitch," she said.

"Can't argue with you there," the ghost said.

Teagan looked at her and waited.

"What?" the ghost asked.

Teagan shrugged. "So . . . are you gonna tell me that this is somehow my fault too?"

"Omigod! Have you really not figured this out yet?" the ghost said, dropping her hands at her sides dramatically.

"What?" Teagan asked.

"It's a wonder I ever made it through high school," the woman said. She slid forward on her chair and looked up at Teagan, staring into her eyes. "I am you, Teagan. You are me."

An uneasy sense of recognition shot through Teagan, but she scoffed. "Please. That's not possible."

"Before tonight would you have believed that anything you've seen was possible?" the ghost asked patiently.

"But you can't be me!" Teagan said, pushing herself away from the wall. Her mind reeled as her heart went into spastic palpitations. "You . . . you don't look anything like me!"

"Three chin surgeries, a nose job, and a lot of lipo can change a person," the ghost said.

"A . . . a nose job?" Teagan asked, touching her face. "But I like my nose."

"Until some loser frat boy tells you it's perfectly triangular your senior year at college," the ghost said, leaning back in her chair. "You don't react very well to that."

Teagan covered her nose with her hand. She stared at the ghost, trying not to see the resemblance, but now she couldn't avoid it. Those eyes were obviously hers. And she had that tiny birthmark next to her right ear. And the infinitesimal dot at the top of her left ear from that ill-conceived eighth-grade piercing.

But still, it was too bizarre to wrap her brain around. She couldn't have been talking to *herself* all night. The idea was just too freaky. Even considering everything that had happened.

"I want proof," Teagan said, struggling to remain calm.

The woman got up and walked over to a leather purse sitting on the counter. Teagan felt numb as she watched the ghost rifle through it and pull out a wallet. She flipped it open and held it out. Teagan looked down at the New York State license. There was a picture of the ghost, looking pissy, and next to it was the name Teagan Lauren Phillips. It had her birth date right on it. This was, in fact, *her*.

Teagan gripped the countertop with her free hand. "How is this possible?"

She dropped the wallet and turned around, trying desperately to line up everything she had seen and heard today in her mind, but none of it seemed to connect. Just thinking about it made her head hurt.

"How . . . how could you be me?" she asked, facing the ghost again. "You're, like, *old*. I couldn't have grown up to be you. You told me I'm already dead."

The ghost grimaced apologetically, pressing her teeth together. "Yeah, well, that was kind of a little white lie."

Teagan felt like the entire world had tilted beneath her. For a moment her vision blurred. She curled her hands into fists and willed herself not to physically implode.

"*What?* WHAT!!??" she screeched, not even giving herself time to be relieved. "A *little white lie?* You *told* me I was *dead*! How can you do that to somebody?"

The ghost backed away slightly. "Well, when you think about it, you're me, so I kind of did it to myself. And that's not *so* bad!"

Teagan sputtered, at a loss for words. "What? I just . . . I can't. . . . How can you . . . ? What did you . . . ?"

"Look, I had to tell you that you were dead or you never would have taken all of this seriously," the ghost explained. "But the good news is, you're still alive! You're just on another plane of existence. You have a chance to change almost everything you've seen tonight."

Teagan braced her hands against the countertop again and tried to breathe. *I'm not dead. I'm not dead,* she repeated over and over. *I can still talk to my dad. I can still tell off Lindsee and Max. I can still do so many things. . . .*

She was feeling lighter and headier by the second.

"I'm not dead," she said aloud, standing up straight. Her lips twitched into a smile.

"No, you're not," the ghost said, taking her hand. "At least, not yet."

Teagan opened her eyes and found herself staring down at a corpse. The ghost's corpse, to be exact. Chin bandage and all.

"Oh God!" she said, taking a couple of steps back.

The corpse was lying in a silver casket, the top half of which was open. A light placed in the ceiling shone down on her face, giving her an eerie glow and highlighting her sunken cheeks. Teagan glanced up at the ghost, who was staring grimly down at her dead self.

"That's you," she said, her mouth completely dry. "I mean, it's . . . it's us. Oh God. It's *me*."

"Yep," the ghost said blandly.

"How can you stand it?" Teagan asked, her heart pounding with fear. Why in hell would the ghost bring her here of all places?

"It *is* a little weird," the ghost said.

"This is too creepy," Teagan told her, gripping her purse strap with both hands. "I'm outta here."

She turned around and froze instantly in her tracks. Everything inside her seized up. The room was full of empty chairs, all lined up to face the casket. Sitting in the very first row was Teagan's father, staring bleary-eyed at the body. Next to him was Karen, who clutched his right hand in both of hers. Next to *her* was a young girl of about thirteen with curly blond hair and a bored expression.

"Oh my God. Dad," Teagan said, breathless. Her eyes instantly welled with tears and she spun around yet again. She slammed right into the ghost. "Why are you doing this to me?" she wailed. "Haven't you put me through enough already?"

The ghost didn't answer. She had gone pale and waxy, clearly having trouble with her own emotions. Teagan, being barefoot while her future self was wearing heels, found herself staring right at her chin bandage. She swallowed in disgust and as her eyes trailed down, they finally fell on the necklace that hung low on the ghost's chest. Teagan's heart slammed. She narrowed her eyes. Hanging on a silver chain was a round, clear crystal with about a zillion tiny edges. They caught the light and sent sparkling rainbows all over the room.

"Where did you . . . get that?" Teagan asked, mesmerized. She had seen this necklace before. She *knew* this necklace.

The ghost looked her in the eye. "My father gave it to me," she said. "For my sixteenth birthday."

Teagan's eyes fluttered closed and she stumbled backward into an empty chair. Everything inside her dropped to its lowest point. Blindly she groped for her purse and pulled it onto her lap. She only opened her eyes again when she had managed to undo the clasp.

There it was. Nestled amid her hairbrush and spray gel and her extra thong. A small square box, wrapped in red paper.

Quaking like an over-caffeinated supermodel, Teagan ripped off the paper and pried open the lid of the small blue velvet box. Even though she knew what she would find, she still felt like her life was flashing before her eyes. The small round crystal her mother had worn every day of her life.

"I always thought she was buried with it," Teagan said, her eyes brimming. "I never thought I'd see it again."

The ghost reached past Teagan into her purse and pulled out the card. Teagan couldn't move but wouldn't have stopped her if she could. She was hypnotized by the necklace as memories of her mother came pouring back. Her mom wore this very necklace around her neck. This necklace actually lived with her mom every single day.

"Dear Teagan," the ghost read. "Your mother wanted you to have this on your sixteenth. She would have been so proud."

Teagan felt a wry laugh bubble in her throat. "At least that was what he thought this morning," she said.

Ghost Teagan scoffed as well. "Yeah."

Teagan slumped back in her chair and gazed at the casket. There was no way she could wrap her mind around all of this. She couldn't believe she was looking at her future self—her future corpse. She couldn't believe she was sitting here talking to her own ghost. How had all of this happened? And why? Teagan had never even been sure if she believed in ghosts or an afterlife. Now she found herself wondering if her mother had somehow had something to do with this. There were about five billion questions she could have asked the ghost.

Where did she end up going to college?

Did she ever get married?

Did Max and Lindsee end up in some horrible, disfiguring car crash?

But there was only one question on the tip of her tongue.

"How did we die?" she asked quietly.

Ghost Teagan pointed to her chin bandage. "Freak accident during our third chin reconstruction," she said.

Teagan's jaw dropped. She was horrified. "Was that the surgery I just watched you schedule?"

"Yep," the ghost said with a nod.

"But the doctor *told* you it was dangerous!" Teagan said. "Why did you do it?"

"Well, the older I got, the more my self-image consumed me," Ghost Teagan said, crossing her arms over her chest. "All I'd been focused on for the last eight years or so was remaking myself."

"But you had to have a job. Friends. A life," Teagan said. "Right?"

"I did have a job. I worked at Calvin Klein."

"Really?" Teagan squealed.

"Did pretty well, actually," Ghost Teagan said. "I was one of their youngest executives till I cashed in my stock options last year and retired."

"You retired so young?" Teagan said, stunned. "Why?"

"All those surgeries and workouts and treatments and nutritionists take up a lot of time," the ghost said wryly.

"Oh my God," Teagan said, slumping further. "You're a total freak."

"No. *You're* a total freak," the ghost said. "At least you will be if something doesn't change. No matter what I did to my body, I was never satisfied. Do you know why?"

"Why?" Teagan asked, staring at the waxy skin on the body in front of her.

"Because my problem was never on the outside. It was on the inside," Ghost Teagan said, turning in her seat. "Do you remember the first question I asked you tonight?"

Teagan closed her eyes and rubbed at her forehead, so overwhelmed she felt like she might collapse. "No."

"I asked you if you knew why you were so angry," the ghost said. "So. Do you?"

Teagan swallowed. "Um . . ."

"I'll tell you. It's because you're mad at your mom. You're mad at her for leaving you and you're mad that you never got to have a real family after her death," the ghost said. Teagan's insides ached. "Well, there they are," the ghost said, throwing a hand across the aisle toward Teagan's father and Karen and the odd little girl. "They're right in front of you. But if you keep pushing them away, you're never going to shed that anger."

Teagan took a deep, shaky breath and forced herself to look across the aisle at her dad and his wife. Age and sorrow had deepened the wrinkles in her father's forehead and around his mouth. He was going gray near his temples. His shoulders were slumped in grief. When he squeezed out a few tears, Teagan tore her gaze away, afraid her heart might not be able to handle it.

"Who's the girl?" she asked, checking out her lovely profile.

"That's our sister," the ghost said.

Teagan didn't know how many shocks she could take. "We have a sister?" she said.

"Yep. She's thirteen years old," Ghost Teagan said. "Cool kid, too. Not that I ever cared," she added under her breath.

Teagan barely heard her. She stood, placed the jewelry box inside her purse, and put it down on the chair. Now that she knew who the girl was, there was no looking away. Teagan stepped over in front of her and took in her beautiful blue eyes and smooth skin. She had Karen's hair and nose and her dad's mouth. Teagan knew if she saw the girl smile, she would see a replica of her very own grin. Although with the ill-fitting black sweater and baggy black pants, she clearly hadn't inherited Teagan's sense of style.

"I can't believe I have a sister," she said.

"Can we go now?" the little girl asked suddenly. "I hate this."

Teagan's face fell.

"Have some respect for your sister," Karen scolded.

The girl crossed her arms. "She hated me," she said. "She was so mean to me."

"Honey—"

"No! Seriously, Mom. Don't you even know that's why I always hide in my room when she comes over?" she said. "She was scary."

"Ugh!" Teagan cried, indignant.

"No, it's true," the ghost told her. "I was like hell on wheels around her. Around everyone, actually."

"But I've always wanted a sister," Teagan said, stunned. "How could I possibly treat her that badly?"

"Because by the time she was old enough to know you, it was your only way," the ghost said. "You never appreciated her."

"She never acted like I was her sister," the girl said sadly. "She only ever acted like I was some freak who irritated her and—"

"Tree! That's enough!" Karen whisper-yelled.

Teagan flinched. "They named her *Tree*?"

"I know," the ghost said, rolling her eyes.

"I'm gonna wait in the car," Tree said, grabbing her bag and stalking out.

Teagan watched her go, devastated. She should have been best friends with that girl. She should have taken her shopping and gone for facials with her and hosted sleepovers. Instead the girl clearly hated her with every fiber of her being.

"This sucks," Teagan said.

"Tell me about it," the ghost replied, glancing at her own corpse.

"I guess we should go too," Teagan's father said, looking around the deserted room. "It doesn't look like anyone else is going to show up."

Teagan took in the emptiness of the place for the first time and shivered. "No one came?" she asked, her voice a near whimper.

"Who was going to come? All the people I've bitch-slapped over the years?" the ghost asked.

"This isn't funny!" Teagan shouted. *"You're* dead! We're dead! And everyone hates us! We were an awful, horrible, sad, mean person. No one even came to our funeral!"

Teagan's father pushed himself shakily out of his chair and Karen slid her arm through his.

Desperation shook Teagan from the inside out. She felt to the very core of her soul that she couldn't let her father leave this room. That she couldn't let him go. Yet there was nothing she could do about it. It was over. He was alive and she was dead and clearly neither of them had ever said a word to each other. Neither of them had ever made their feelings clear.

"Dad! No!" Teagan shouted, tears spilling over. "Don't leave me here! I need you. I . . . I love you, Dad. I don't want to be dead!"

He and Karen approached the casket slowly and Teagan watched as her father leaned forward, squeezed his eyes shut, and kissed the cold forehead of his daughter.

"Good-bye, my sweet girl," he said, tears wetting the corners of his eyes.

"Dad! No! Come on!" Teagan cried. "Don't say good-bye. Take me home, Dad! Please! Don't leave me here! I just want to go home!"

Her father turned his back on her, slipped his arm around Karen's shoulders, and walked out.

"Dad! Daddy!" Teagan wailed. "Dad! Come back!"

"Teagan—" the ghost said.

"Shut up!" Teagan shouted, near hysterics. "I want him back! This isn't fair! Dad!"

But he was gone. Teagan deflated completely. She collapsed over the end of her own casket and bawled uncontrollably, her chest heaving up and down. Her fingertips clawed at the slick silver surface of the box, making awful squealing noises as they gripped and slipped.

"This can't be it," she said through her tears. Her heart was racked with pain. "This can't be how I end up. I'm supposed to have a future! I can't die like this! I can't be all alone!"

She felt a hand on her back and looked up into her own eyes. The ghost's face was wet with tears. She handed over Teagan's purse.

"Teagan," the ghost said regretfully. "It's time to go."

"Go? Go where?" Teagan asked.

"It's gonna get worse before it gets better," the ghost told her.

"Worse?" Teagan croaked. "How can it possibly get worse than this?"

The ghost touched Teagan's shoulder grimly, her eyes filled with sorrow. "This time, you'll have to go alone. . . ."

Interview with Teagan Phillips re:
Upcoming Sweet Sixteen Party
Transcript 4, cont'd.

Reporter: Melissa Bradshaw, Senior Editor,
Rosewood Prep *Sentinel*

MB: So, you mentioned presents. Anything specific you're hoping to unwrap that night?

TP: You're not really going there, are you? I
mean, you did listen to the other kid's tape
by now.

MB: Let me rephrase. What *material goods* might
you like to take home that night? What's on
Teagan Phillips's wish list?

TP: Wow. Got a few hours?

MB: (*laughs*) How about a top five?

TP: Okay, let's see. I want the new Dior bag—
the one that's supposedly not available until
the fall but that I know certain friends of my
father are able to acquire. I *need* those new
Seven leather jeans with the studding down the
seam. *So* cute. I've gotta get a whole new set
of skis, poles, boots—the works—for Vail next
year. My stuff is so last year.

MB: I don't mean to interrupt, but I thought

you said real women don't do sports or something.

TP: Skiing doesn't really *count*. Does it?

MB: I'm sure the Olympic ski team would beg to
differ.

TP: Oh. Right. Touché.

MB: I think you have two more top-five gifts.

TP: Two more? All right. I want a sixty-inch
plasma screen for my room so my friends and I
can have proper movie screenings without any
of the staff traipsing through. And I *definitely* need a bigger bathroom. You barely have
room to properly blow-dry in there.

MB: I'm sorry, you want someone to give you a
new bathroom?

TP: Well, half my dad's friends *are* in con-
struction.

MB: (*under her breath*) At least you're not
asking for your own helicopter.

TP: Oh! That would be so cool! Can I change my
answer?

Chapter 15

Teagan found herself standing, alone and trembling, in a very familiar room. She wiped at her eyes and took a few shaky steps away from the wall to place her hands on the back of a dining room chair. She knew every corner of this room as if she had never left it.

"Oh God," she said aloud, her breath quickening. "This is my . . . house." The house she and her father had moved out of after her mother had died.

She looked around for the ghost, but she wasn't there. Why hadn't she come along? Didn't she want to *see* this?

Hugging herself, Teagan slowly looked around, taking it all in. She saw the sideboard full of her grandmother's Tiffany china. The Mission-style table and chairs her father and mother had picked up on a trip to North Carolina. The stain on the woven rug where she had spilled grape juice as a child. The thick green curtains she had hidden behind for her father's surprise thirty-fifth birthday party. She could see the nose and fingerprints on the windowpanes where she used to press her face and hands, looking out to the street, waiting for her father to come home from work.

The dining room was decorated for a party. A pink-and-white paper tablecloth covered the table, and pink Barbie plates were set up at every chair. There were pink plastic knives and forks, clear plastic cups, and tons and tons of confetti. Streamers clung to the light fixture at the center of the room and draped across to every corner, secured with Scotch tape. There were pink and white balloons tied to every chair. At the head of the table, two place settings were topped by two gold crowns. One for Teagan. One for Emily.

"Mommy! Mommy!"

Teagan's heart seized and she whirled around. Across the entryway in the living room, hundreds and hundreds of ribbons curled down from hundreds and hundreds of balloons. A dozen or more kids sat in a circle where the coffee table would normally be, sifting through crumpled wrapping paper and boxes of toys. Parents milled about with drinks and cameras, looking on with amused pride. There was laughter, screeching, talking, and some kind of kiddie music playing in the background.

Suddenly Teagan saw herself around age six run across the open doorway, brown curls streaming behind her, and disappear on the other side. The little girl was followed seconds later by a tall boy with choppy brown hair. Emily's brother, Gary, around age eight.

Teagan's pulse started to rush so loudly in her ears, it was deafening. This couldn't be the year she thought it was. This couldn't be happening. She had wished for it so many times over the past ten years, the very thought that she was about to see what she thought she was about to see made her quake from the tips of her ears all the way down to her toes.

Somehow, she had no idea how, Teagan made herself move. She stepped, barefoot, onto the cool, smooth wood surface of the entryway and instantly remembered sliding across it in socked feet for hours with Emily, slamming sideways into the door and laughing the whole way. She glanced at the coatrack next to the window and saw her father's old trench hanging there next to her mother's white rain jacket. Her heart pounded more and more frantically with each step. It seemed like an eternity passed before she was standing at the doorway to the living room. But then she was there and time stopped.

"Mom," Teagan whispered, all of her breath leaving her.

Her mother was there. Right there. Sitting in the chair and a half, surrounded by ribbon curls that bounced around her shoulders. Her blond hair was pulled back in a low ponytail and she wore a light green sweater with beading all around the collar. Her green eyes crinkled at the corners as she smiled at the crazy present opening that was happening at her feet. Her face was thinner than Teagan remembered, but what was most overwhelming was how very much she looked like Teagan did today. The same high cheekbones. The same wide forehead. The same pointy chin. The chin that Teagan would adore from here on out. She had never realized she had gotten that from her mom.

I can't take this, Teagan thought. Her heart actually felt like it was going to burst.

"Mom?" Teagan said, her voice cracking as she stepped into the room. Her mother didn't look up, but that didn't stop Teagan. God, she had imagined this moment so many times. What she would say if she had one more chance. Now that it was here, all she wanted to do was crawl into her mother's lap and hug her. All she wanted to do was sob all over her mother's shoulder. If she could just touch her. Just once . . .

"Mommy! Look!"

Little Teagan jumped up from the circle of kids, a hot pink boa from a dress-up set she had received as a gift wrapped around her neck. She raced right past Teagan and hurled herself into her mother's lap. Her mother let out an "oof" but laughed and gathered the little girl into her arms. Gary quickly followed, hovering near the arm of the chair and saying nothing.

As her mother smothered little giggling Teagan with kisses and hugs, Teagan's heart welled up with envy. That was *her* mother. Those were *her* hugs. That kid in her lap was so clueless. She didn't even know the woman was about to die. But Teagan had been waiting for this moment for ten years. She deserved this moment.

"Lauren?"

Teagan's mother looked up and Teagan followed her gaze. Her father was standing in the opposite doorway, the one that led to the kitchen. He looked almost exactly the same, just a little less wrinkled around the eyes. He and Teagan's mother exchanged a silent look of understanding and then Teagan's mom placed little Teagan on the floor. She was wearing a light blue T-shirt with daisies embroidered around the neckline and a matching skirt with a daisy trim. Classic mom-picked outfit. The lady did love Teagan in blue.

"Why don't you and Emily go get your picture taken with Barbie?" her mother suggested, whispering in little Teagan's right ear.

Teagan felt a shiver go down her right side at the very thought of her mom being that close to her.

"'Kay. Emily!" little Teagan shouted.

Up popped six-year-old Emily, braids, freckles, and all, from the floor, where she was busy playing with a Crayola arts set. She wore pink overalls, a pink-and-white-striped shirt, and pink sneakers. Little Teagan held out her hand and Emily took it. Together they picked their way over boxes and bows to the teenager standing in the corner, dressed up as Genie Barbie, posing with little Jennifer Robbins for parental photos. Gary, of course, trailed behind.

Jennifer stepped away from Barbie and in stepped Teagan and Emily to pose with the impersonator. Teagan still had that picture somewhere. At least she thought she might.

Teagan could not for the life of her figure out what she was doing here. The ghost had told her it was going to get worse before it got better, but this was great. Maybe she couldn't hug or talk to her mother, but she was right there in the flesh. Teagan's lifelong wish was coming true. The one thing she wanted more than all the material crap on her birthday list *combined*. How could this be bad?

Teagan's mother got up and crossed the room to her dad. Teagan pushed herself away from the wall and followed the couple as her father slipped his arm around her mom's shoulders and held her tight. They walked through the little entryway to the kitchen, past the pantry and the door to the basement.

"Are you sure you're up to this?" Teagan's father whispered.

"I'm sure," her mom replied.

Then they all stepped into the kitchen together. Two parents and their invisible future daughter. Sitting at the table on the far side of the kitchen, hunched over and in tears, was Marcia Lupe, Teagan's nanny.

"I sorry, Miss Phillips," Marcia said, shredding a soaked tissue all over the table. "I so, so sorry. I didn't mean to hurt you or Mr. Phillips."

"What's going on?" Teagan asked. Of course, no one answered.

Teagan's mother sighed and sat down diagonally across from Marcia. She placed her thin, frail hand on top of Marcia's healthier one. Teagan's mom attempted to look into the older lady's eyes, but she ducked her head so far down it was impossible.

"We're not angry, Marcia," Teagan's mother said in a soothing voice. "I just want you to talk to me. What happened? Why did you take the money?"

Teagan blinked. Money? What money?

"I know it's only for emergencies," Marcia said, sniffling. "But I thought I'd be able to pay it right back."

"What happened, Marcia?" Teagan's mother asked patiently.

"It's Tomas's school," Marcia said, wiping her eyes. "They took part of his scholarship away. He didn't do anything wrong," she said quickly. "They said there were budget cuts. He needed five hundred dollars for rest of semester or he couldn't come back next year. Senior year! I only had three hundred. I took the money for the other two."

Teagan's mother and father looked at each other. There was so much empathy in her mother's eyes that Teagan welled up all over again. She couldn't believe this. She couldn't believe that Marcia had *stolen* from her parents. Part of her was waiting for them to freak out all over the place, but another part of her was wishing and hoping they wouldn't. This was Marcia. She *needed* Marcia.

"I get a second job to pay you back, but the first paycheck won't come for two weeks," Marcia said, tearing up all over again. "I'm so sorry; I know you will have to fire me."

Teagan's mother squeezed Marcia's hand. "Oh, Marcia. We're not going to fire you," she said.

"What?" Marcia asked, shocked.

"I just don't understand why you didn't come to us instead of taking the cookie jar money," Teagan's mom said. "You know I would have given you an advance. Especially if you needed something for Tomas. I'm a mother too, you know," she added with a smile.

Marcia smiled back. She stood up and the two women hugged.

"Next time just talk to us, okay?" Teagan's mother said to her. "I understand how hard things can get. And Teagan loves you. You can't leave us. Especially not now."

"Teagan is a lucky girl to have a mother who loves her so much."

Teagan's mother bit her lip. She was clearly fighting back tears. "Thank you."

Marcia's eyes welled with tears for Teagan's mother. "Thank you. Both of you. I won't forget."

As Marcia left the room, Teagan's dad enveloped her mother in his arms. He kissed her forehead and looked down into her eyes. There was no mistaking his expression—total and complete love.

Teagan's mother smiled in reply just as the doorbell rang. "I'll get that," her father said. Then he gave his wife another kiss and walked out.

Teagan's mother took a deep breath and started for the living room. She was just passing by Teagan and the ghost when she suddenly wavered and her knees seemed to give out.

"Mom!" Teagan shouted, petrified. She lunged for her mother, but her mom slapped her hands into the wall, stopping herself before she could fall to the ground.

"Mommy?" Teagan heard herself say, tears stinging her eyes.

Slowly Teagan's mother turned her head. She stood up and looked right at Teagan. They were the exact same height. Teagan was looking directly into her mother's green eyes.

"Omigod, Mom. You see me," Teagan said, a tear slipping down her cheek.

Then her mother's brow creased in confusion and she shook her head. Smoothing her sweater down, she turned around and walked back into the living room. Teagan, with nothing left to do, leaned against the wall and sank down to the floor in tears, dropping her purse on the tile. The pain in her chest was unbearable. If she could have ripped her own heart out to stop it, she would have.

"Okay, I get it now," Teagan said, pressing the heel of her hand into her forehead as she sobbed. "You're trying to show me that Mom was a good person who didn't fire people and I'm just an asshole, right? Because I got Emily's aunt fired."

She gazed after her mother, her vision swimming. Nausea overwhelmed her as she realized what her mother would think of the way she had acted tonight. Catherine had spilled cocktail sauce on Teagan and gotten canned. Her mother hadn't even fired Marcia for *stealing*.

She would be so ashamed of me, Teagan thought, her face heating up. *She would hate me.*

Teagan turned her attention toward the party, where little Teagan was passing out her gifts to all of her friends, letting them open the boxes and play with the new toys. Teagan had no recollection of ever doing that. She couldn't even imagine letting someone else play with her stuff before she did. Was that really her in there?

"Here. I'll give you a bow," little Teagan said to Emily. She pulled a striped ribbon out of her costume set and tied it around the bottom of one of Emily's braids. Gary, meanwhile, sat at little Teagan's side, tightening another of the ribbons around his index finger until the tip turned purple.

"Teagan? Can I play with this?" Jennifer asked, holding up a pink Barbie Corvette.

"Go ahead," little Teagan said with a shrug. She grabbed another ribbon and started working it around Emily's other braid.

Jennifer Robbins always broke everything she got her hands on, Teagan thought, amazed. But little Teagan didn't seem to care. She just looked like she was having fun.

Teagan watched as her father lifted little Teagan up and swung her around. Little Teagan squealed and laughed, tilting her head back and trying to grab as many balloon ribbons as possible. Her mother, seated back in her place, laughed as well.

"Whaddaya say we do our dance number?" Teagan's father asked, placing little Teagan on the floor.

"Yeah!" little Teagan cheered.

Her father went over to the CD player and cued up a new song. She saw him crank up the volume and instantly Stevie Wonder's "You Are the Sunshine of My Life" filled the room. Teagan's father turned around and started grooving back toward little Teagan in a totally cheesy way. Little Teagan clapped and laughed.

Teagan's tears welled up all over again as she remembered how her twelve-year-old self had so callously dismissed this tradition. And look how much her father clearly reveled in it. He sang along with Stevie—badly—grinning as he lifted little Teagan onto his feet and started dancing her around the room.

"God, no wonder he thinks he failed with me," Teagan whispered. "I was so mean to him later."

She watched her young self singing along and swinging her hair and loving every minute of her father's attention. She looked up at him like he was some kind of god. Like no other man in the world existed. And the love was just as evident on her father's face. Just as clear as day.

The song ended and all the parents in the room applauded. Teagan watched as her father twirled little Teagan one last time and deposited her in her mother's lap. Her mom lifted a slim box from the end table next to her and handed it to little Teagan.

"This is from me," she said.

Little Teagan's eyes widened in awe.

"Do you know why you're getting this present?" Teagan's mother asked.

"'Cuz I'm six today!" little Teagan announced.

"That's true," her mother said. "But it's also because you are the most lovely, generous, big-hearted girl in all the world. And I love you."

Teagan snatched a tear away from her eye. She refused to cry again.

Little Teagan ripped open the gift and revealed a Gucci box. From inside she unfurled a colorful paisley silk scarf. "Oooooh!" she said, sliding it around in her hands. "It's so slippery!"

Teagan's mother laughed. "Do you like it?"

"Yeah," little Teagan said with a nod.

She didn't get it. She didn't get that the gift was too sophisticated for her. She didn't know that her mother was only giving it to her because she knew that she was dying. She knew that she would never have the chance to give an older Teagan a gift like that. It wasn't until years later, the scarf tucked under her pillow, that Teagan had realized what her mother had done. She had tried to give Teagan a last birthday gift that she could keep for a lifetime.

Little Teagan draped the scarf around her shoulders and her mom tied a little knot in it to keep it there, like a cape. Little Teagan smiled at her mom. She reached up and touched the necklace around her mother's neck.

"Can I wear the magic necklace?" she asked. *"Please?"*

Teagan's mother touched the pendant resting against her chest. "I don't know," she answered, tilting her head. "Only a very special person can handle the magic this necklace holds."

Magic, Teagan thought with a rush of realization. *That's right. She always said that necklace was magic.* Was that why her own ghost had come to her tonight? Because her father had given her this necklace? For the first time all night Teagan wished the ghost was there with her. She was the only one who could answer these questions.

"I'm a very special person!" little Teagan announced.

"That's right!" her mother said, feigning surprise. "You are!"

"What kind of magic does it have?" Emily asked, leaning against the side of the chair along with ever-silent Gary. "Does it blow stuff up?"

"No! Nothing like that!" Teagan's mother said, reaching around to unclasp the necklace. "It helps you see things that no one else can see."

"Like invis-dible things?" little Teagan asked, keeping her eyes trained on the pendant.

"Sort of," her mother said, cradling the necklace in her palm.

Little Teagan, Emily, and Gary leaned in and stared down at the necklace like it was glowing. They were obviously in awe.

"So can I wear it?" little Teagan asked.

"Of course you can," her mother said.

She placed the necklace around little Teagan's tiny neck and it hung down over the scarf, practically to her belly button. Little Teagan picked it up and smiled. Her mother gathered her up and hugged her to her chest tightly. Teagan's heart split wide open, wishing that was her—*present-day* her. She wanted that hug. She had never wanted anything more.

"Oh, my sweet one," Teagan's mother whispered to her, trying to hold back tears. "Never change. Promise me you'll never change."

Teagan couldn't take it anymore. She got up and started across the room. She was going to rip that little kid out of her mother's arms and take her place if it killed her.

She took one step and the ghost appeared in front of her, expression stoic, her back to the living room.

"No!" Teagan cried, realizing. "No! Don't!"

But the ghost grabbed her arm and in a rush of warm wind, Teagan's mother faded before her eyes.

"You can't do this to me!" Teagan wailed tearfully. "Take me back! I want to see my mom!"

But she was alone again. Her ghost had disappeared once more. Teagan recognized her parents' room instantly. The light-blue-and-white-striped wallpaper. The delicate white curtains. The light yellow accents on the bed. The black-and-white photographs of beach scenes—crashing surf, reeds blowing in the wind, a seagull standing on top of a pylon. Teagan's mother loved the beach. They had kept a house at the New Jersey shore when Teagan was very young. It was the first thing her father had sold after her mom died. Teagan had always resented him for that. She knew that her mother would have wanted them to keep going there together. To enjoy her favorite place.

Now Teagan's father sat on the edge of the bed and removed his shoes and socks. He was wearing the same clothes he had worn to the party. The only light in the room came from the open door to the adjoining bathroom.

"It was a lovely party, wasn't it?" Teagan's mother said, stepping into the light. She rubbed moisturizer over her hands and arms. In her flimsy white nightgown she was all skin and bones. Her mother's obvious frailty took Teagan's breath away. Already she was losing ground to the cancer.

"Everyone had a great time," Teagan's father said. "Come here and sit. You look tired."

Teagan's mother smiled slightly. "I am tired. I'm always tired."

She was shaky on her feet as she crossed to the bed and sat down. The dark purple circles under her eyes were highlighted by the near translucence of her skin. Teagan almost thought she could see the white of her mother's cheekbones showing through. Either the party had completely ravaged her mother, or she had been wearing a lot of makeup earlier that day. She looked like a different person.

"Did you see her today?" Teagan's mother said. "She

handed out cake to everyone else before she would even take a bite."

"She's an amazing kid," her father agreed, taking her mother's hand.

"I'm so proud of her," Teagan's mom said, her eyes welling up. "She's such a sweetheart." She took a deep breath and looked into her husband's eyes. "Do you think she'll hate me after I—"

"Shhh. Do not finish that sentence," Teagan's father said. He leaned forward and kissed her forehead, then her cheek, then her mouth. "She will never hate you. I will make sure that she knows exactly what an incredible woman her mother is."

"Was."

His face contorted like his heart was breaking.

"You have to get used to using the word *was*, Michael," Teagan's mother said.

"Don't say that," Teagan's father insisted. "I don't want you thinking that way."

Teagan's mother took a deep breath. "Michael, I—"

She paused, and what little color she had left her. Her eyes bulged and she was suddenly on her feet, running for the bathroom.

"Lauren?"

The retching was loud and intense. Teagan closed her eyes and turned toward the wall, but she couldn't shut down her imagination. In her mind she could see her mother doubled over, her tiny body racked with pain as she threw up, her delicate fingers clinging to the towel bar. She had seen it so many times as a kid. All that fear came rushing back to her—the confusion, the uncertainty. Just like that, Teagan was a scared six-year-old again.

"Lauren."

"Don't come in here!"

Teagan's father was on his feet, but he stopped in the center of the room when his wife shouted at him. He looked like a little kid being shouted at by a teacher. So small and scared.

"Why are you showing me this?" Teagan shouted to no one, tears squeezing from the corners of her eyes. "Haven't you tortured me enough already?"

The water ran in the bathroom and Teagan heard her mother gargling. A moment later she stepped out again and smiled apologetically at her husband.

"All those years of dieting and now I would give anything to be able to eat one meal and know I was going to keep it down."

Teagan's stomach turned. Her father stepped up to his wife and ran his fingers gently through her thinning hair. "Chemo sucks."

"Chemo sucks," her mother repeated, then grinned as if spitting out those words made her feel better. Teagan couldn't believe her parents could joke at a time like this.

It's what got them through, a little voice in her mind said. *Joking about the awfulness. It's what got them through it all.*

"Let's get you to bed," Teagan's father said, reclaiming Teagan's attention.

He leaned down and lifted her mother into his arms like he was lifting a small child. Teagan's heart caught so hard she instinctively held her hand over her chest. She had never seen her father do anything so intimate and kind. Her mom leaned her head on his chest and draped her arms around his neck until he deposited her in the bed. He pulled the covers up over her legs and sat at her feet.

"Can I get you anything?" he asked.

"No. I just want to sleep," she said. "Promise me you'll never let Teagan become a diet fiend like her dear old mom."

"Lauren—"

"I want her to enjoy life. I want her to love herself. I want her to realize every day how beautiful she is," Teagan's mom said, sliding down under the covers.

"She is," Teagan's father said. "And so are you. I think she would be damn lucky to turn out just like her mom."

Teagan's vision swam with unshed tears. She wanted so much to be like her mother, but the more she saw, the more she realized she was anything but. All her mother wanted in the world was to be able to keep her food down and Teagan spent half her time trying *not* to eat.

I'm everything she didn't want me to be, Teagan realized. *I'm a huge, disgusting disappointment.*

"Take me out of here!" Teagan shouted at the ceiling, tears streaking down her face. "Please! I get the point, all right? I'll be a better person! I'll be the person my mom wanted me to be! But please! I need to get out of here!"

Finally the ghost appeared in front of Teagan and placed her hand on her arm.

Interview with Teagan Phillips re:
Upcoming Sweet Sixteen Party
Transcript 4, cont'd.
Reporter: Melissa Bradshaw, Senior Editor,
Rosewood Prep Sentinel

MB: Well, you seem pretty confident that this party is going to rock fairly hard. Any concerns?

TP: No. None. I'm ready.

MB: Really? You're not worried that the chef won't show or the pictures won't come out or the makeup artist will be going through her Ronald McDonald phase?

TP: Missy, Missy, Missy, I have everything planned down to the letter. I had all my contracts notarized. I haven't paid a single one of my vendors their full fees and I won't until they deliver everything on time and in impeccable order. Trust me. Nothing can possibly go wrong.

Chapter 16

Teagan tried to quiet her sobs, shivering as she felt herself re-form once again. She was petrified. Scared to open her eyes and find herself . . . where? At another funeral? Watching someone else she had devastated without even realizing it? Reliving more horrors from her past?

"Seen enough?" the ghost asked.

Teagan heard a rumble of thunder and opened one eye. She was back in the country club's basement. Upstairs, the music pounded. Someone let out a loud whoop that was followed by a universal cheer. People were having fun.

"Sorry I couldn't go with you, kiddo, but I wasn't sure I could handle all that," the ghost said.

"Mom must be so disappointed in me," Teagan said. She was so ashamed she could barely speak. "Wherever she is, she's looking down on me and frowning."

"Not just you," the ghost said. "Us."

Teagan swallowed. Nodded. Wished there was a place she could curl up in a ball and just disappear.

"But you can change all that," the ghost said firmly. "You can change who you are. Who you'll become. You've been given a second chance."

Teagan felt a little fluttering in her heart. "I . . . I have," she said slowly, shivering all over. "I'm not dead. I . . . I have my whole life in front of me."

"Yes! Yes, you do!" the ghost said, her eyes wide. "And you *have* to change it. You *will* become *me* if you don't do something *now*. I was rich, yeah. Stinking, filthy rich. But it didn't matter. I was also bored almost every day. And very, very lonely. Do you realize that not one person acknowledged my last birthday on earth? Not one! I alienated everybody. I cared for no one and as a result, no one cared for me!"

Teagan held herself against the onslaught of goose bumps as she watched the ghost start to pace in front of her.

That's me, she thought, shivering. *That's who I become.*

"You have to do something, Teagan!" the ghost ranted, opening her hands to the sky. "You have to change now, before it's too late. You have to start appreciating the people in your life. The ones that matter—not the shallow morons like Max Modell. Who cares about freakin' Max Modell? What did he really mean to you? I mean, *really*? All you cared about was being seen with him. All you cared about was that he was the hottest guy in school. I mean, if you actually cared one iota about him, you would have been devastated when you saw him with his tongue down Lindsee's throat. You would have been heartbroken! But what did you say when you saw them?"

"I . . . uh . . ."

"You pointed out that Lindsee's butt was bigger than yours!" the ghost shouted. "Do you realize how shallow that is?"

Teagan looked at the floor. Normally she would be royally pissed if someone spoke to her like that, but now she found herself smiling. Starting to laugh. How ridiculous was she? Was that what she had *really* said? She thought about Max and realized that the idea of being without him didn't really bother her at all. It was when she thought about him with Lindsee that her skin started to prickle. She was concerned about the competition, not the guy.

"You have to forge some real relationships, Teagan," the ghost said, squaring off in front of her. "You need a little depth in your life or else it's not really a life. It's just a fashion show. And let me tell you something about fashion shows. Once they're over, ninety-nine percent of the people who witnessed them forget every single thing they've seen."

Teagan swallowed hard, thinking of the turnout at her funeral. It seemed everyone had forgotten her before she had even died.

My funeral. My lame, deserted, sad funeral. Teagan knew she would never forget what she had seen in her future. It would never stop giving her chills.

"Okay," Teagan said, standing up straight. "I get it."

"Do you?" the ghost asked shrilly.

"Yes! I swear! I get it!" Teagan shouted.

She grasped the diamond heart around her neck and ripped it as hard as she could, breaking the delicate chain. She tossed the heart on the floor, dug through her purse, and came out with her mother's necklace. Her fingers fumbled, but she was finally able to secure it around her neck. The second the cool crystal touched her skin, she felt calm. She felt confident. She felt happy.

Teagan smiled at the ghost. Slowly the ghost smiled back.

"I get it," Teagan said calmly.

The ghost nodded. "You know, I actually think you do."

"Is this why you came to me tonight?" Teagan asked, touching the necklace. "Did Mom send you?"

"I don't know," Ghost Teagan said with a smile. "But I hope so."

The two Teagans stared into each other's eyes. Suddenly Teagan was overwhelmed by all the things she wanted to say. She wanted to thank the ghost. She wanted to apologize to her. She wanted to tell her that she wouldn't let her down. They weren't going to be dying before they ever had the chance to really live. Not anymore. Everything was going to change.

Teagan took a deep breath. "I—"

"I know," the ghost said with a serene smile. "After all, I'm you, aren't I?"

Teagan grinned. The ghost lifted her hand in a wave. At that moment the door to the basement opened, accompanied by a bright flash of lightning and a deafening crack of thunder. When Teagan's eyes readjusted to the darkness, the ghost was gone. Just like that.

"Teagan! Are you down there!?" her father shouted.

"Right here, Dad!" Teagan shouted back, her voice cracking.

Teagan let one single tear slip down her cheek as her father barreled down the stairs. She looked up at the ceiling and smiled. In her entire life, she had never felt so light.

"Teagan! Oh my God! Are you all right?" her father asked.

Teagan turned around and threw herself into her father's arms. She was alive! She could actually hug her father! This was something she would never take for granted again. Her father hugged her back tentatively, clearly surprised by the force of his daughter's sudden embrace.

"What happened to you?" her father asked.

"I'm so sorry, Dad," Teagan said. "I'm so sorry for everything. I don't want you to be disappointed in me anymore. You didn't fail me or Mom or anyone."

"What?" her father asked, baffled.

Teagan pulled back and touched the crystal on her chest. Her father saw the necklace and smiled.

"When you walked in tonight, I . . . I was wondering why you weren't wearing that," he said.

That was why he looked so disappointed when he saw me, Teagan thought. *I was wearing Max's piece of crap instead of Mom's magic necklace.*

"Well, I'm never taking it off now," Teagan told him. "And from now on I'm going to make you and Mom proud. And Karen! Karen too!" she said with a smile. "No more tantrums, no more unauthorized shopping sprees, no more skipping class for three-hour facials."

Her father's brow creased. "You've skipped class for—"

Teagan colored. "Never mind! It's in the past!" she shouted, taking his hand and pulling him toward the stairs. "Come on! We're missing the party!"

She ran upstairs, skipping the knotted step entirely, and emerged into the brightly lit hallway, feeling like she was actually coming back from the dead. Everything looked prettier to her now—brighter—less confined. She took a deep breath and twirled around in her bare feet, almost knocking right into Mrs. Natsui. The maid was out of breath and her arms were full of slippery dry-cleaning bags.

"I'm so sorry, Miss Teagan! There was a huge accident on Slippery Rock Road and it took forever to get here," Mrs. Natsui said.

"An accident?" Teagan asked. "Was anyone hurt?"

Mrs. Natsui blinked and looked past Teagan at her father. Teagan saw her dad shrug in confusion.

"I . . . I don't think so, Miss Teagan," Mrs. Natsui said. "Thanks to the rain, no one was traveling too fast."

"Oh, good," Teagan said. "I'm glad you're okay."

Now Mrs. Natsui looked like she was about to call in a team of neurologists. "Are *you* okay, Miss Teagan?"

"I'm fine," Teagan said with a smile. "Great, actually!"

"Okay," the maid said, clearly unconvinced. "I brought the dresses."

"Don't need 'em! I am not going to be one more second late for this party," Teagan said, grabbing the shorter woman's shoulders and spinning her around. She hustled her down the hall toward the bridal suite. "Dump 'em in there."

Mrs. Natsui eyed the horrible stain on Teagan's dress. "Are you sure you don't—"

"Please. I have to wear this dress. Do you have any idea how much this thing cost?" Teagan said. "Just drop 'em."

Mrs. Natsui did as she was told, dropping her load on the divan near the door. All the dresses slid off the velvet cushions onto the floor, a pile of sequins, chiffon, and silk.

"Good. Now, have you eaten tonight?" Teagan asked Mrs. Natsui, throwing her arm over the maid's shoulders. "Let's go get you some filet mignon. Unless you don't eat meat. Do you?"

"Oh . . . um . . . yes, Miss Teagan," Mrs. Natsui said.

"Call me Teagan," she said. "I've had enough of this miss crap. I mean, you've seen me in my underwear, right?"

"Yes, miss. I mean, Teagan," Mrs. Natsui said, finally smiling.

"There ya go!"

Teagan started off down the hall toward the ballroom, the maid scurrying to keep up with her long strides. She glanced over her shoulder at her father, who was frozen in place.

"Come on, Dad!" she shouted. "It's time to dance!"

Teagan burst through the double doors into the ballroom and a couple of guys from her class covered their mouths as they cackled at her, but all she could do was smile. It was nice to be seen again, no matter how frightening or hilarious she might look.

"Dad, wait for me here," Teagan said at the edge of the dance floor.

"Oookay," her father replied, slipping his hands into his pockets.

Teagan stopped one of the passing waitresses. "Would you mind getting a filet mignon for my friend over there?" she asked, pointing at Mrs. Natsui, who was standing, looking uncertain in her maid's uniform, next to a table full of Oscar de la Renta devotees.

The waitress smiled and nodded. "Sure."

"Thanks!" Teagan called after her.

Teagan noticed Maya and Ashley sitting at an otherwise empty table, three seats away from each other, both still in black. Maya tapped a fork on the table monotonously while Ashley twirled a strand of hair around her finger and stared into space. Teagan rolled her eyes and walked over to them.

"Come on, you guys! It's a party!" Teagan called out.

Ashley's jaw dropped when she saw Teagan. Maya sat up straight. "Teagan! What happened to your dress?"

"Don't worry about it," Teagan said. "Listen, back in the bridal suite are a bunch of my favorite dresses and none of them look anything alike. Why don't the two of you go back there, get changed, and then get your butts back out here? I'm about to get this party started."

Maya almost fell off her chair. "Really? You're lending us your clothes?"

"They're just clothes!" Teagan said.

Ashley looked at Maya, considering. "Well, we *did* get our colors done."

"Apparently I'm a spring and Ashley's a fall," Maya informed Teagan.

"Great! See? I knew I hired those overpriced fashion experts for a reason," Teagan said. "I'm sure there's something you'll like back there. Now go."

Evidently her friends were smart enough not to second-guess her too much. They both got up, squealing with glee, and took off.

"Oh, and hey! You guys!" Teagan called after them.

Maya and Ashley stopped and turned around. Their eyes nearly bugged out of her heads as Teagan enveloped them both in a group hug.

"Thanks so much for my present. It was awesome," Teagan said. "You guys are good friends."

"You're welcome," Maya said, surprised.

"Yeah. Anytime," Ashley added with a smile.

They turned and headed for the bridal suite and Teagan took a deep breath and looked up at Shay, who held one earphone to his ear as he hit a button on his laptop. This was going to be interesting.

Teagan ducked around the dance floor, feeling dozens of eyes trained on her—and not in the good way to which she was so accustomed. She knew they were all taking in her destroyed dress, her frizzy hair, the blackened soles of her bare feet. But none of it bothered her. Looking so disheveled in public was rather freeing. What did it matter, as long as she was here?

"Hey! Beckford!" Teagan shouted, walking up behind him.

Shay turned around, startled, and guffawed. "What happened to you?"

"A lot, actually," Teagan said, putting a hand on her hip. "Listen, do you have this old song called 'You Are the Sunshine of My Life'?"

"Stevie? *You* want to hear *Stevie Wonder?*"

"Do I really need to go over which one of us is the boss?" Teagan said lightly.

Shay rolled his eyes but smiled. "All right, all right. Yeah, I got some vintage Stevie here somewhere."

"Good. I want to dedicate it to my father, okay?" she said. "Oh, and could I borrow your microphone? I'd like to make an announcement."

"It's all yours," Shay said, handing over the mike. He turned down the volume on the speakers and started typing into his laptop. The activity on the dance floor slowed as everyone turned toward the DJ with interest.

"Hi, everyone!" Teagan called out. "Can I have your attention, please?"

The room grew hushed as the people at the tables and

milling around the room turned their attention to the birthday girl.

"I would just like to thank all of you for coming to my sweet sixteen," Teagan said. "I hope everyone is having as much fun as I am."

There was a round of cheers and hollers. Melissa Bradshaw snapped a few pictures, as did Roly-Poly Man.

"I would also like to thank George Lowell and the staff for all the hard work they put into making this evening a success," Teagan continued. "I really appreciate everything you've done and all the sacrifices you've made," she added, thinking of George's outfit and the firings. "So thank you."

She saw a couple of the waitresses exchange an impressed glance.

"Oh, and waitstaff, you can take off those ridiculous sunglasses now," Teagan added. A few of them cheered as they tossed the $250-a-pair specs aside. Teagan tried not to cringe. They were just things, right? Not important.

"Of course, there is one person who made this whole night possible," Teagan said, looking for her father on the dance floor. "The man who makes everything in my life possible—my dad."

"Aw!" the crowd cooed on cue. The people on the dance floor turned and parted around her dad. He stood alone in the back corner of the dance floor, looking sheepish and pleased.

"Dad, thank you for everything you've given me," Teagan said. "I know we both wish that Mom were here with us tonight, but thanks to this beautiful gift, I feel like she *is* here," Teagan said, touching her new crystal. Her father's eyes swam with tears. "So now, if you don't mind . . ."

"We're all set," Shay whispered, flashing Teagan a thumbs-up.

"Dad," Teagan said, her heart thumping, "this song's for you."

Stevie Wonder's voice filled the room and Teagan's father grinned hugely.

"You are the sunshine of my life! That's why I'll always stay around. . . ."

Teagan walked back down the steps, cocktail sauce stain and all, and met her father in the center of the dance floor. She stood on her tiptoes and opened her arms. Somewhere inside her there was the old fear of rejection, the tiny voice of doubt that sounded a lot like her twelve-year-old self. She took a breath and squelched it.

"May I have this dance?" she asked her father.

"Thought you'd never ask," he replied.

Teagan smiled as her dad led her around the floor, spinning her out, then back in. She felt like she was being warmed from her head to her toes and knew that her mother was smiling down on them. She knew it as surely as she knew that this was a birthday moment she would remember for the rest of her life.

"What happened to you down there?" Teagan's father asked, curious.

"I think I got knocked out, and I had this insane dream," Teagan replied, knowing that the truth would freak him out. "It was the future and my life pretty much sucked. So when I woke up, I decided to change it."

"Interesting dream," her father said. "I never thought I would say something like this, but I'm kind of glad my daughter clunked her head."

Teagan laughed. "Me too."

"Of course, it might be a good idea to take you to the hospital," he said. "Get you checked out."

"Yeah, that would be a *great* idea. But later," Teagan said. "For now I just kind of feel like dancing."

"Your wish is my command," her father said with a smile.

As her dad twirled her around the dance floor, Teagan caught a glimpse of Karen standing on the periphery, smiling as she looked on. She adjusted the strap on her designer dress and grasped at the sides, wiggling to pull the skirt down. The woman was obviously uncomfortable in the skintight frock—a dress that was so un-Karen and that Teagan now understood had only been worn for *her* benefit. Teagan's heart skipped a beat when she thought of how horribly she had been treating Karen. Karen, who clearly loved her dad. Who would one day make an incredible mom.

"You know, Karen is really an amazing person," Teagan told her father.

He smiled. "Yeah. She is."

"She's always nice to me, even though I'm so mean to her. I'm so sorry."

Her father sighed. "She understands, honey. It's hard for a girl to see a new woman in her father's life."

"Dad, I'm not a baby anymore," Teagan said. "I'll stop acting like one, but you've gotta agree to stop thinking of me as one."

Her father regarded her with a flicker of respect in his eyes. "Agreed."

"I'm happy that you found her," Teagan said, a small lump forming in her throat. It was true, but it was still difficult to swallow her pride and say it. She would have to get used to the sensation. "And I know Mom is happy for you too."

The last strains of the song started to fade away and Teagan's father gathered her up in his arms and hugged her tightly, lifting her off the ground. Teagan hugged him back, squeezing her eyes closed.

"Let's have a hand for the birthday girl and her father!" Shay called out, even though most of the guests were already applauding.

"Thank you, Teagan," her father said in her ear.

"Thank *you*," she replied. "I love you, Dad."

"I love you too, sweetie," he replied.

Her father returned her to the ground and held her hands as she pulled back. Teagan couldn't stop grinning for all the world. Things were going to be different now. She could feel it in her bones.

"I have to go," Teagan told him, releasing his hands. "There's something I have to do."

"But you really just got here," her father said, shouting over the now-raucous music.

All around them, Teagan's friends from school poured back out onto the dance floor. From the corner of her eye, Teagan saw Maya now sporting the blue Vivienne Tam and Ashley shimmying along in the flowered Gaultier. For the first time all night, they both looked like they were having fun.

"I know, but I have to leave," Teagan said.

"Teagan, I know we just agreed that I should stop thinking of you as a baby, but should I be concerned?" he asked.

Teagan laughed. "Mom would want me to do what I'm going to do. Trust me."

Her father smiled. "All right, then. I'll see you at home later."

Teagan honestly couldn't remember the last time she had

heard her father utter that phrase. It made her heart hurt with longing and relief all at once.

"See you there," she said.

On her way off the dance floor, Teagan grabbed Karen and hugged her tightly. Karen was so stunned she tripped backward and nearly knocked them both off their feet.

"Whoa! What's that for?" Karen asked, laughing.

"It's for making my dad happy and for coming here tonight and for breakfast this morning," Teagan said. "Thank you. Really. For everything."

Karen shrugged and smiled, looking as confused as everyone else had since Teagan had returned from her psychedelic journey. "You're welcome," she said.

"So . . . what's up with the dress?" Teagan asked, looking Karen over.

"Oh, you don't like it?" Karen said, placing her hand over her stomach.

"No! It's totally cool. I love it," Teagan said. "It's just not you. At all."

Karen laughed. "That's about right. I just thought it would be appropriate, you know. High-fashion party and all that. I didn't want to embarrass you."

Teagan flushed and looked at the floor. "You don't have to do that," she said. "You don't have to dress to impress me. My dad likes you the way you are. Loves you, actually."

Karen beamed. "That's sweet of you to say."

"You're pretty cool when it comes down to it," Teagan said with a nod. "I mean, the earth mother thing never goes out of style—as long as the person wearing it isn't a poseur, which you are *definitely* not."

"Okay," Karen said, blinking.

"But Karen, 'Tree'? Really?" she said, leaning in. "Why don't you go with Lily or Rose or something? Something that won't get her butt kicked on the playground. Think about it."

She clapped Karen twice on the shoulder, then walked off, leaving her father's fiancée looking even more baffled than ever.

Interview with Teagan Phillips re:
Upcoming Sweet Sixteen Party
Transcript 4, cont'd.

Reporter: Melissa Bradshaw, Senior Editor,
Rosewood Prep Sentinel

MB: Okay, how about this. If you couldn't have a sweet sixteen party—

TP: Missy! Bite your tongue!

MB: No, I'm serious. If the lavish bash and the perfect dress and the munchable DJ and all that stuff were not an option—

TP: Can I just go on record as pointing out that *I* never said Shay Beckford was munchable?

MB: Fine. Noted. Anyway, if all that were not an option, what would you be doing on your sweet sixteen?

TP: Killing myself?

MB: Come on.

TP: All right, fine. I'll play your little game. (*sighs*) I guess if I *had* to come up with another scenario, I'd just want Lindsee and Max to be there. Whatever we were doing. They are, after all, the most special people in my life.

MB: Really?

TP: Why is that so hard to believe?

MB: Oh, it's not, I guess. It must be nice to have people you love so totally.

TP: (*pause*) Oh, well, I do. I love them both. We're like *this*.

Chapter 17

Teagan was on her way back to the DJ booth when a familiar giggle stopped her in her tracks. Her breath caught as Max and Lindsee staggered out from behind one of the raised stages set up for the models, looking flushed and happy. They sprang apart the second they saw her.

"Teagan!" Lindsee said with a false grin.

"Backstabbing slut!" Teagan replied in the exact same chipper tone.

Lindsee went pale. Teagan could have sworn the volume on the music went down a touch. She could practically feel Shay watching her from behind. Fine by her. The more witnesses to this, the better. Lindsee and Max had tried to make a fool of her tonight. Now it was her turn.

"We weren't doing anything!" Lindsee protested, clearly not realizing her MAC Ruby Woo was smeared all across her cheek. Max really could be a sloppy kisser sometimes. That was one thing about him Teagan was not going to miss.

"We were just—"

"Deciding exactly what Max should say when he shot me down tonight?" Teagan asked, turning her raised eyebrows on her boyfriend.

Max had the decency to look momentarily appalled and snagged. But then he let his shoulders fall and adopted his normal hot-boy demeanor. Slight slouch, one hand in pocket, head tilted like he was just *so* cute he could not be denied.

"Come on, princess. You know it's not like that."

Teagan took a step closer to him. "Oh, I know *exactly* what it's like. Let me save you from burning the brain cells you'll need to string the appropriate letdown together. I wouldn't have sex with your silk-boxer-sporting self if you ingested a lifetime's supply of super-strength Viagra." She looked at Lindsee. "Which, I'm sure you've already discovered, he *will* need."

The handful of students milling around the scene gasped and laughed. Max's mouth opened and closed a few times, like a fish gulping for water. Teagan realized that it was quite possible that the poor boy had never been insulted in his life. He had no idea what to do.

Good. It was always nice to make history.

"Oh, and Lindsee? I know you said you wanted something sparkly, so the diamonds, if you're interested, are in the storage cellar," Teagan said. "I've been given something much better," she added, placing her hand on her chest over the crystal. "Later."

Teagan flipped her hair over her shoulder and took the steps up to the DJ booth. She smirked as she thought about the dark stairs and that scary knotted step. Maybe Lindsee was in for a little ghostly encounter of her own. If not, at least she'd have a nice big bump on her head come tomorrow.

Okay, so Teagan was supposed to be turning over a new leaf, but a girl had to stick up for herself.

"Nice tongue-lashing," Shay said as she arrived at his side. "Remind me never to piss you off."

"Speaking of, I have a favor to ask," Teagan said.

"Looking for a little Chaka Khan now?" Shay asked.

"Chock-a what now?" Teagan asked.

"Never mind," Shay said, amused.

Teagan got the distinct feeling he was laughing at her, but she swallowed her pride and chose to ignore it. Not snapping back was torture, though. This being a better person thing was going to take some work.

"I was just wondering if you'd be able to fit my gifts in your van. I mean, if the food you slipped out of here isn't taking up too much room," Teagan said.

Shay blinked and looked over his shoulder. "How did you know about that?" he asked, leaning toward her. He smelled of sweat and suede. It made Teagan flush.

"I have eyes everywhere, my friend," she said coolly.

"Okay, that's scary," Shay said. "But yeah, I think I have the room. Why?"

"Good. I need you to help me load it up and then I need you to drive me somewhere," Teagan said.

"Problem number one, you didn't hire me to be your chauffeur," Shay said. "Problem number two, I'm kind of in the middle of the job you *did* hire me to do."

"Trust me, you'll want to do this," Teagan told him. "And if you're worried about the DJ'ing duties, why don't you just let the busboy finish the party? You were going to let him sub in anyway."

Now Shay looked positively freaked. She could see his

Adam's apple going up and down. "Did you have a security system installed in here?"

"Shay, Shay, Shay," Teagan answered, shaking her head and smiling wickedly. "You underestimate me. Now, you deal with DJ Busboy. I gotta go find George."

"He's right there," Shay said, pointing.

Sure enough, George was walking hurriedly past the DJ booth toward the kitchen. "Hey, George!" she shouted.

He stopped instantly, spotted her, and snapped to attention.

"Meet me by the presents in five," Teagan told Shay, starting down the steps.

"Yes, Your Highness," Shay replied.

Teagan stopped, ignored the shiver that ran through her, and took a breath. "Please," she said, turning to face him. "Meet me in five, please."

Shay looked her up and down, impressed. "Maybe the sweet sixteen really does signify a passage into adulthood."

Teagan rolled her eyes and approached George Lowell.

"Miss Phillips?" he said. "Is there a problem?"

"Actually, there is," Teagan began. "It's about that woman you fired. . . ."

"Oh, sweet ketchupy relief."

Teagan let out a luxuriant sigh and leaned back in her folding metal chair, starting to feel semi-human again. Her toes were cozy and warm in a pair of brand-new white sweat socks, courtesy of the East Sheridan homeless shelter. All around her in the huge basement gym/cafeteria of the old Catholic school that served as the refuge, families gathered around tables, handing out the bags and bags of food that Teagan and Shay had bought on the way over. Between all the burgers and fries and the hors d'oeuvres from the party, it was a haute-cuisine-meets-hoedown kind of meal. Everyone was going to bed full tonight.

Over in the back corner, Cora Martin—the shelter's director—and a few of her staff members gushed and gasped as they tore into Teagan's tremendous stack of gifts. Designer clothes and bags were piled everywhere. All electronics— MP3 players, portable DVD players, watches, and the like— were laid out on a table. A middle-aged woman with a frizzy ponytail lifted a pair of red Manolo Blahniks out of a box and gave them to a preteen in denim overalls. The girl shoved her tube-socked feet into the couture shoes and started teetering around on them. Teagan shook her head and looked away. She could only imagine the gasps of horror her friends would chorus if they were to witness such a travesty.

Shay sat down across the table from her and grinned as he opened the wrapper on his own fried chicken sandwich.

"Are you sure about this?" he asked. "You don't have to donate *all* of it."

"Do you realize those shoes are worth four hundred dollars?" Teagan said, lifting her chin toward the girl

Shay whistled.

"What could four hundred dollars buy around here?" Teagan asked.

"Food for one of these families for over a month," Shay said.

Teagan glanced over his shoulder at the father and two small children at the next table. The little boy was making designs in his ketchup using a french fry. The girl was pulling pickles off her sandwich and laughing as she put them on her father's burger. Her dad smiled and kissed the top of her head. Teagan's heart felt all tingly just watching them.

"Yeah, I don't need it," Teagan said, returning her attention to her meal. "*This* is what I need," she added, taking another huge bite of her cheeseburger.

"Excuse me . . . I hate to bother you," Cora said, joining them. She was a short, powerfully built woman with spiky gray hair. Her smile revealed one gold tooth and a completely kind soul. She held a stack of checks in her right hand along with a pen. "Here are the checks for you to write over. If you still want to, of course. There's a lot of money there. A lot."

Teagan sat up straight, slid the checks in front of her, and started to sign. She didn't even want to think about money or clothes or any of it anymore. For once she wanted to think about something that really mattered.

"I have to say, we've never had a windfall like this before," Cora said. "You're going to be talked about at this place for months to come."

Teagan smiled. That morning all she had wanted was for her party to be talked about for months to come by all the students at Rosewood. But she had a feeling that being remembered around the shelter would be much cooler.

"Here you go," Teagan said, handing over the stack of checks.

"Thank you so much," Cora said. "If there's ever *any*thing we can do for you . . ."

"I'll keep that in mind," Teagan said with a smile.

Cora surprised Teagan by leaning down and giving her a huge bear hug. "You are a true angel," she said before returning to her work.

"Hear that?" Teagan asked, beaming. "I'm an angel."

"All right, Phillips, spill it. What's with the Princess Diana act?" Shay asked, shifting forward in his seat. "What happened to you today?"

Teagan groaned. "Please don't ever call me 'princess.'" Shay raised his eyebrows and Teagan shrugged helplessly. "It's a long story," she said finally.

"I got nowhere to be," Shay said. "Tonight's gig kind of fell through."

Teagan laughed and rested her arms on the table. "Fine. Let's just say I had a visit from someone tonight. Someone who made me realize that my current attitude wasn't really leading me anywhere good."

"Who was it? The ghost of Christmas future?" Shay joked.

"No!" Teagan blurted. "Nothing like that! It was just a . . . an aunt! A distant aunt who showed up for the party and kind of gave me a talking-to."

Shay smiled. "Well, I'd like to meet this aunt sometime," he said, looking Teagan in the eye. "Sounds like my kind of girl."

Teagan suddenly felt warm all over. "Maybe you will someday."

The longer Teagan held Shay's gaze, the hotter her skin grew. He didn't look away. Neither did she. God, he really *was* munchable. What would it be like to kiss him? What would it be like to cuddle up in his arms and nuzzle his chest with her face? Was she really engaged in a flirtatious stare-down with Shay Beckford, man of a thousand veiled insults?

Oh, man. I really hope I was always wrong about him and he actually can't see through me, Teagan thought. Now would be a really bad time for him to read her thoughts.

"What're you thinking?" Shay asked with a smirk.

Oh, thank God!

"What are *you* thinking?" Teagan countered.

"I asked you first."

"I asked you second."

"Are we really going to go there?" Shay asked.

"*You* went there," Teagan pointed out. "I just followed."

Shay broke into a heart-stopping grin and sat back in his chair. "You so like me."

"Yeah? We'll see about that," Teagan said, grinning uncontrollably.

From the corner of her eye, Teagan saw one of the shelter workers hold up a gorgeous light pink cashmere sweater and was hit with an idea. An idea so utterly perfect, she was shocked she hadn't come up with it before. She *had* always displayed a certain talent for perfect ideas.

"I'll be right back," she said, pushing herself up from the table. "I think I see one thing I might want to keep."

"And the consumer is back, ladies and gentlemen!" Shay announced to the room, throwing his arms up.

Teagan laughed. She turned to walk backward in her socked feet. "Oh, Shay. How little you know me."

Interview with Teagan Phillips re:
Upcoming Sweet Sixteen Party
Transcript 4, cont'd.

Reporter: Melissa Bradshaw, Senior Editor,
Rosewood Prep Sentinel

MB: So, tell me. What's it really like working with Shay Beckford?

TP: (*clears throat*) It's fine.

MB: He was kind of the BMOC around here. I bet he has a hard time taking orders from a sophomore.

TP: Well, Missy, you just have to know how to handle the help.

MB: You know how to handle Shay Beckford.

TP: Oh, I've got him right where I want him.

MB: So those legendary baby blues have no effect on you.

TP: (*pause*) None whatsoever.

Chapter 18

Shay's vintage Dodge van shuddered as he pulled it to a stop at the curb on a familiar tree-lined street. The rain poured down in buckets, battering the thin roof so hard that Teagan was certain it was about to collapse. Now that all the booty had been removed from the cargo area, the sounds reverberated and echoed and made it so loud inside the van that she could hardly hear herself think.

Or was her beating heart drowning everything else out?

"Is this it?" Shay asked.

Teagan had never felt this nervous in her life. As she leaned forward and looked up at the pathway leading to the front door, she grasped the gift bag's ribbon handles in her sweaty palm and quadruple-guessed herself. Earlier tonight she had seen firsthand what lay beyond that door. Did she really want to go in there?

"Teagan?"

"Yeah. This is it," she said, sitting back her seat. Her legs stuck to the cracked vinyl and her feet sweated inside the new Christian Dior sneakers she was sporting—the only other gift she had appropriated from the stack, and only at Shay's insistence.

"Are you going in?" Shay prompted.

"Just give me a second, would you?" Teagan asked.

"Sorry."

She took a deep breath and screwed up her courage. After everything she had seen tonight, she knew in her heart that this was something she had to do. She also knew that she had to do it now, while everything was fresh in her mind, or she would lose her nerve. Somehow knowing all this didn't make getting out of the van any easier.

"Well, this has been an interesting night," Shay said finally.

"You have no idea," Teagan replied, staring at the front door of the house.

"I have an idea from what I've seen," Shay told her, studying her face. Teagan finally looked at him and saw the uncertainty in his stunning blue eyes. If she didn't know any better, she would have thought he was feeling almost as nervous as she was. "Can I say something that might sound a little strange?"

Teagan turned in her seat a bit to face him, crooking her leg under her. "Trust me. Almost nothing could seem strange to me right now."

"Okay, then. I wanted to say . . . that I'm proud of you," Shay said.

Teagan's first instinct was to laugh, but she quelled it as soon as she felt the undeniably pleasant response her heart was having.

"You're proud of me?" she said, smiling slightly.

"Yeah. I know we hardly know each other, so I don't really

have any right to even say that, but what you did tonight . . ." He looked through the windshield at the pitch-black night and his brow furrowed as if he was choosing his words carefully. "I know what you did tonight was a huge sacrifice for you. Leaving your party early, giving away all that stuff. And after breaking up with your boyfriend—it had to be a rough night."

"Oh, it was. But Max had nothing to do with it," Teagan said.

"Yeah?" Shay said.

Teagan shook her head. She didn't want him thinking she was heartbroken or on the rebound or anything. Just in case. "Hardly even a blip."

"Well, that's good," Shay replied with a grin. "But anyway, I was kind of honored to be a part of the whole thing. Thanks for taking me along."

He reached over and brushed a lock of hair behind her ear. The touch sent a shiver of pleasure down her side. Shay looked at her—really looked at her—for the first time.

Teagan smiled slowly. It was a total kiss moment. She knew it and so did he. But suddenly, thanks to him, she felt more than able to pick up this gift bag and go ring that door-bell. If this night was going to be about someone other than Teagan, she had to go. Now. Even if it meant giving up her only chance with Shay.

"Well, thank you," she said, breaking his gaze with a her-culean effort. "I guess I should go."

"Yeah. Okay," Shay said, blinking as if he was coming out of a trance.

"Thanks for everything. For driving me around and all," Teagan said. She popped open the door and was assaulted by the thick, humid air outside.

"Hey," Shay said. "Can I call you sometime?"

With that one question Teagan knew that there would be another kiss moment. Maybe many more. Teagan tossed her frizzed-out hair over her shoulder and smiled.

"You better."

Seconds later, Teagan and Emily were face-to-face for the first time in two years.

"Teagan?" Emily said, her eyes wide.

"Hi!" It was pretty much the only word Teagan remembered at the moment.

"Omigod! Are you okay? Come inside!"

Emily grabbed Teagan's arm and hauled her over the threshold. Behind her, Teagan heard the sound of Shay's van roaring away. A couple of Emily's more-curious friends bounded over to the small entryway. Teagan saw them go into shock, then listened while they giggled and reported back to the kids in the living room.

"You're soaking wet," Emily said.

"I brought you something," Teagan said, holding out the two bags. Emily, in classic Emily fashion, went for the grocery bag first out of clear curiosity. She cracked up laughing when she saw what was inside.

"Cheetos and OJ," she said, grinning. "You remembered!"

"Yo! Birthday girl! Who was at the do . . . ?"

Gary loped into the room and paused when he saw Teagan dripping on the hardwood floor. He crossed his arms over his chest and clucked his tongue, obviously amused.

"Well, look what the cat drug in," he said in a fake Southern accent. "Teagan Phillips herself."

"Gary, stop being a moron and go get Teagan something to wear," Emily said, rolling her eyes.

"Whatever you say, birthday girl," Gary replied. "But that only counts for today, remember."

He turned and bounded up the stairs, which creaked under his weight.

"So, what are you doing here?" Emily asked Teagan, laying the bag of snacks on the floor. "Don't you have some big party going on?"

"Yeah, but I ditched it," Teagan replied. "I realized I didn't want to be there. I realized that those people were . . ." She paused, feeling hot and completely unworthy. Why was this so hard to say? "We should be together on our birthday," Teagan said finally. "That's why I'm here."

"Wow," Emily said, nodding. "I don't think I've ever been this surprised."

Teagan smiled. "I seem to be making history a lot tonight."

At that moment Emily's mother stalked in from the kitchen, her face already boiling red.

"What the hell do you think you're doing here?" she demanded, squaring off with Teagan. She wiped her hands vigorously on a towel and then balled it up as if she was going to throw it at Teagan's head.

"Mom!" Emily exclaimed.

"Mrs. Zeller, I—"

"You have a lot of nerve coming into this house after what you've done tonight, Teagan Phillips," she said. "Now, I know you lost your mother and I'm sorry for that, but it doesn't give you a lifelong pass to act like a spoiled child."

Teagan swallowed hard and stared at Emily's mother. On some level, she felt like this was exactly what needed to happen.

"I know," she said quietly.

A door upstairs opened and Emily's aunt Catherine descended the steps slowly, hugging her sweater to herself. She looked absolutely stricken to find the central character in her current nightmare standing at the bottom of the stairs. Gary followed her, a pair of jeans and a gray sweatshirt in his hands, but he had the intelligence to hang back.

"Now I hope, for your mother and father's sake, that you figure all this out before it's too late," Mrs. Zeller said, her skin slowly returning to a normal shade. "Otherwise I have no doubt about how you'll end up."

For a long moment everyone was quiet. Emily watched Teagan uncertainly, clearly wondering if she was just going to bolt or throw a fit. Teagan simply took a deep breath and looked at Emily's mother. She wondered if her own mother had been around for the past few years if Emily's mother would have said the same thing to her. She had a feeling she would have.

"I'm sorry. You're right," Teagan said finally, her pulse racing. "Everything you just said is absolutely true."

There was a stirring in the living room as Emily's friends reacted to this. Mrs. Zeller couldn't have looked more stunned if Ed McMahon had just walked in with a million-dollar check.

Teagan turned to Catherine, who clenched her jaw and eyed her stoically.

"I'm truly sorry for what I did to you earlier," she said. "I was totally out of line and I want you to know that George Lowell should be calling you. Soon. Tonight, hopefully."

The phone rang and Catherine exchanged a look of disbelief with her sister. She ran down the last few steps and together they headed for the kitchen phone.

"Well. This party just got a little more interesting," Emily said.

Relieved, Teagan laughed and looked down. Only then did she realize she was still clutching the gift bag.

"Oh! Here! I know you already opened all your presents, but—"

Emily took the bag, a quizzical expression on her face. "How did you know that?"

Teagan shrugged and watched as Emily pulled the pink cashmere sweater out of the bag.

"Whoa," she said, rubbing the cushy fabric between her fingers. "This is the softest thing I've ever felt."

"I hope pink is still your color," Teagan said.

"Totally," Emily said, holding the sweater against her chest. "Teagan, I love it. But you didn't have to—"

"Yeah, I did," Teagan said, pleased.

Emily reached over and hugged Teagan—rain, cocktail sauce, and all. "I'm so happy you're here," she said.

Teagan closed her eyes against a sudden stinging of tears. "Me too."

There was a systematic pounding on the stairs and Teagan looked up to find Ricky jumping down them one at a time, his face tight with concentration. Gary got out of his way so he could make it down to the floor. Once he got there, he looked up at Teagan curiously.

"Hey, Ricky," Teagan said.

"How d'you know my name?" he asked.

"Yeah. How do you know his name?" Emily added.

Teagan had opened her mouth, her brain scrambling for a response, when Catherine and Mrs. Zeller walked back into the room, saving the day.

"Well, that *was* George Lowell," Catherine said. Was it just Teagan, or had a little color returned to Catherine's cheeks?

"He offered me the promotion!" she announced.

Teagan's jaw dropped.

"No way!" Emily shouted, throwing her arms around her aunt. "Congratulations."

"Yeah, Mom!" Ricky cheered, hugging her legs.

"I couldn't believe it," Catherine said, grinning. She reached down and lifted Ricky into her arms, where he wrapped both his legs around her hips. "He wants me to come in on Monday and fill out all the insurance paperwork and everything. I got a huge raise *and* he's paying me for a full night of work tonight." Catherine turned to Teagan, holding on tight to her son. "What did you say to him?"

Teagan lifted her hands. "Don't look at me! I just thought you were getting your *old* job back."

Everyone laughed and Mrs. Zeller slid her arm around Teagan's shoulders. "You did good," she said. "Sorry for yelling at you before."

"Actually, it was kind of nice, feeling like I had a parent for five seconds," Teagan told her as Catherine started relaying the details of her new job to her niece and nephew.

"Really?" Mrs. Zeller asked.

"Yeah. Just don't let it happen again," Teagan joked.

"I can't believe I'm actually wearing this," Teagan said. She pulled away the elastic strap on her gold birthday crown and let it snap back. "Ow!" she cried, rubbing her chin.

"Nice one, brain trust," Gary said, slapping her on the shoulder as he walked by the end of the table with the cake knife.

Emily laughed and adjusted her own crown. "Why? You feel stupid?"

"No, not that," Teagan said. In fact, she felt more comfortable than she had all day in Gary's cozy Penn State sweatshirt and Emily's jeans. "It's just . . . been a while."

"Eh. Not *that* long," Emily said.

Her boyfriend, whose name had turned out to be Adam, sat down at Emily's other side and lifted his disposable camera. "Smile, ladies."

Emily slung her arm around Teagan's neck and pulled her close for the picture. They both grinned, then blinked against the flash's shadow.

"Nice one," Adam said.

"So, Teagan, what do you think they're doing over at your party right now?" Jennifer asked, leaning her elbows on the table.

Teagan checked her watch. By now the cake had probably been cut. Max and Lindsee were probably getting busy in some tasteless, semi-exposed corner of the room. The models had most likely revolted and were now dancing with the hot senior boys. It was quite possible that the rest of the younger guests, accustomed to parties with free-flowing alcohol, had overthrown George Lowell's regime and raided the liquor pantry. Meanwhile DJ Busboy was on the mike playing Lord knew what while everyone wondered what the hell had happened to Shay Beckford. All in all, it was probably deteriorating into a disaster.

"You know what, Jennifer? At the moment, I couldn't care less," Teagan said.

The lights dimmed and Emily's mother appeared with a

homemade cake covered in tiny candles. She started off the round of the happy birthday song and everyone joined in, including Emily, who sang Teagan's name, and Teagan, who sang Emily's name. Mr. Zeller snapped pictures with his digital camera.

"Okay, girls! Make a wish!" Mrs. Zeller said as she placed the cake down in front of them. Teagan was touched when she saw that Emily's mother had added Teagan's name under Emily's, writing tiny and at an angle to fit it.

Teagan reached out under the table and took Emily's hand. Emily looked at her, surprised. Teagan grinned back and then they both turned to the cake and closed their eyes.

I wish for a better future than that crap fest I saw tonight, Teagan thought. *And since it's my sweet sixteen, I think I should be entitled to an extra. So I also wish that Catherine lives a long, happy life and never falls off the wagon. Oh! And I also wish that my dad and I will be closer and that he and Karen will be happy and that Shay Beckford will actually call.*

She opened her eyes and saw that everyone was staring at her. Oops.

"Ready?" Emily asked.

"Yeah," Teagan replied firmly.

"One . . . two . . . three!"

They blew out the candles together and everyone applauded. Teagan laughed and sat back in her chair. For the first time in her life, she was absolutely certain that wishes actually mattered. After everything she had been through tonight, there was no doubt in her mind that magic was real. She touched the crystal necklace and looked up at the ceiling, knowing that if her mother had any say in it, all her wishes would come true.

Rosewood Prep Sentinel

SCHIZO-SIXTEEN
Teagan Phillips's Party of the Century: Fab or Freaky?
By Melissa Bradshaw, Senior Editor

Teagan Phillips claimed her high-fashion–themed bash was going to be talked about for years to come, and was she ever right. What started out as a bizarre, tension-filled fete worthy of a tabloid write-up (the birthday girl got doused in cocktail sauce and freaked out, then disappeared; her boyfriend and supposed best friend got a little too hot and heavy on the dance floor) turned into the blowout bash of the decade. And when the last of the delectable cake was eaten and the lights finally came up, Teagan herself had only witnessed about ten minutes of the party she purportedly worked on for over a year.

After disappearing for an hour, presumably to get cleaned up, Teagan reappeared, still stained and now barefoot, to make a heartfelt speech and perform a spotlight dance with her formerly estranged father. She then ripped into Max Modell and Lindsee Hunt for their stunning slut-dom and took off with DJ and Rosewood Prep graduate Shay Beckford for who knows where.

Once the two luminaries (would it be too early to call them a couple?) departed, the party really got going. Some random hottie calling himself DJ Diggler took over the mike and dropped some serious beats for the remainder of the night. The models—hired by Teagan because they were "attractive but not taller or thinner or prettier than [her]self"—came down off their stages and took over the dance floor, "woo-woo-ing" their way into a few hearts. (Rumor has it Marco Rosetti took *two* of them home.) Led by Jimmy Barton, the senior boys managed to locate and break into the champagne fridge and soon the Taittinger's was flowing like it should *always* be. At 1 A.M., when the scantily clad events manager tried to throw everyone out, Maya Thurber and Ashley Harrison handed over their parents' plastic to keep the rager raging.

In the end, fun was had by all, especially those who walked out with new belly button rings completely gratis. This reporter did not partake, though I was pleasantly surprised to find out from certain experts that I *can* pull off a blond chin-length bob and that I am, in fact, an autumn.

ABOUT THE AUTHOR

Kate Brian is the author of the popular *The Princess & the Pauper*, *The V Club* (available in paperback as *The Virginity Club*), *Lucky T*, and *Megan Meade's Guide to the McGowan Boys*. She will always be sweet sixteen at heart.